Night Train to Leningrad

– JOHN C. HAYES –

FASTPRINT GOLD PUBLISHING
PETERBOROUGH, ENGLAND

NIGHT TRAIN TO LENINGRAD
Copyright © John C. Hayes 2008

All rights reserved.

No part of this book may be reproduced in any form by photocopying or any electronic or mechanical means, including information storage or retrieval systems, without permission in writing from both the copyright owner and the publisher of the book.

ISBN 978-184426-584-8

First Published 2008 by
FASTPRINT GOLD PUBLISHING
Peterborough, England.

Printed on FSC approved paper by
www.printondemand-worldwide.com

Foreword

Russia in 1988 was beginning to put on a new face. Words like 'glasnost' and 'perestroika' – openness and reform, were proof that the old dark days of the Cold War were finally at an end. A new age had arrived. But, before such an age could assume some respectable shape, a great deal of cleansing needed to take place. Some of the murky corners of the old order had to be swept out to make way for this brave new world. It would not be easy, for the great cloak of secrecy, which had shrouded everything Russian, would not permit the world to see how such a change was to be achieved.

It is April 10th 1988, and somewhere in Leningrad four people had received letters, hand delivered. Apart from certain details of their private lives, the letters had been instructions for each of them to be aboard the night train for Moscow in two days time. Little else can be revealed for the cloak of secrecy still pervades.

The cleansing process had been set in motion.

John C Hayes

Chapter One
Moscow Station - Leningrad

It is now 12th April and a group of English tourists, mostly schoolchildren, were making their way to the railway station. It was cold but bright and their Russian guide, an attractive woman called Helen, had smugly informed the party that here in Russia they could expect only a maximum of seventy days of sunshine a year. Unimpressed, some wag had quipped that they were lucky if back home they got seventy hours. Nevertheless, the weather was of little concern to the tourists for already they were experiencing the thrill and excitement of an anticipated journey to Moscow, ancient capital of Russia. It was just as well, perhaps that they were unaware of the sinister drama which was to be played out in the last compartment of the last carriage of the night train from Leningrad, else their thrill and excitement would have been tempered with another kind of emotion.

The Moscow Station at Leningrad was, like all large railway stations, full of noise, activity and excitement. Even at ten-thirty at night there was no diminishing of the bustle and clamour. The noises of people coming and going, together with the rattle of long chains of luggage carts, echoed and reverberated into a thousand hollow sounds under a huge girdered canopy. Unlike many stations there was no sign of frenzied panic, which comes with last minute dashes along endless platforms or desperate searches for misplaced luggage. No - none of that, for Russians are an orderly people, a prompt people. They do not miss trains or misplace luggage. If, by some strange chance they do stray in that respect, there is always on hand a multitude of minor officials to shepherd wayward passengers to their proper places. These officials wore armbands to denote their officialdom. Those who actually ran the trains wore a uniform, of course. As in any other country this entitled them to be regarded as petty officials. It was like that everywhere in Russia. Whoever had a job had a uniform of some sort even if that uniform consisted of nothing more than an arm-band worn over their regular clothes. Those who didn't wear any such badge of office were either the workers or tourists. Party officials, especially the secret ones, did not need an armband or any uniform to indicate their profession. They would have exuded a sinister presence however they chose to dress.

Russians are an orderly people certainly, and yet a ripe mixture of types can be seen even in a classless society. There was the student with rucksack on back, scorning the weather by wearing no hat and no substantial boots, though he had a good pair of trainers on his feet. He seemed comfortable enough. He strolled through the barriers with the nonchalance of youth and allowed himself to be directed towards his train. Following close behind was perhaps someone who might be regarded as the more typical Russian. She was a square backed, solid looking woman, whose luggage consisted of a large, bulging bag, which she held with both hands against her chest. The inconvenience did not appear to hamper her in any way and she trundled past the barrier like one who knew where she was going. There were many like her milling about the station.

A waif like creature, a young girl, with a baby cradled in one arm, struggled with her bag of luggage. Russians disdained the use of suitcases it seemed, probably because they couldn't afford them. She continually hesitated as she tried to make up her mind which platform she wanted. Ignoring an offer of assistance from an arm-banded attendant she finally settled on the platform of her choice.

As the station clock ticked its way towards the departure time of the Moscow train, so this ripe mixture of men, women, boys and girls began to swell in ones and twos and even groups. The groups though would likely be tourists for Russians didn't go around in groups.

Nor were all Russians plain and grim looking. They had their fair share of beauty. A smart, attractive woman, with a smart case and smart shoulder bag, pauses as she scans the platforms before making up her mind which one is for her. This woman would stand out in any crowd, particularly a Russian one. Her fur hat is set at a slight, jaunty angle and doesn't quite conceal the blond hair beneath. Her high-heeled boots clack-clack towards her train as she demonstrates that Russian women can be just as elegant as any Parisian model.

The ordinary Russian is not the only traveller tonight, for large groups of tourists, mostly schoolchildren, have now spilled onto the platform, their colourful variety of winter clothing providing a bright, brash contrast to the general drabness of the Russian traveller. Their luggage has already been deposited in a large mountain of cases and bags alongside the waiting train. Having absorbed some of the orderliness of their hosts they proceeded in organised files to this mountain and under the direction of their guides and teachers began to feverishly load cases and bags onto the train. There is no need for panic they are advised, because there is still plenty of time before the night train is due to depart.

Perhaps the tourists were anxious to be doing something to keep warm for the temperature was three degrees below zero. A light, wispy snow had been falling on and off all day, but it was a fine powdery snow, which never stuck on the ground long enough for it to build into any substantial amount. The cold wind, cold for the middle of April, caught the fine powdery whiteness and swirled it around ankles and ears, reminding the unwary or careless, that winter was not done with them yet. Russian travellers seemed not to mind this playful attempt on the part of Nature to convince them that winter was still here. They had already experienced much worse during the icy heart of the Russian climate. This was just an April dalliance with no real threat behind it. The Leningraders were not fooled for they knew that spring was only a week away, two at the most. As they hurried along the platforms which seemed to stretch into infinity they still kept their coats tightly buttoned and their fur hats clamped firmly on their heads. They may not have been fooled by the weather but it was, nevertheless, still very cold.

Among the multitude of echoing noises there was one sound missing. This was a sound now missing from most of the large railway stations of the world and one that would likely not be heard again. For no more was there the grunting and panting of the huge steam locomotives as they came to rest after a long toilsome journey. The sharp hissing bursts of steam as they started off on another journey would never again frighten the old or the frail, nor scald the unwary. They were long since dead. However, there was such an engine reposing in the Moscow station, a mighty black and green leviathan, freshly painted but no longer spouting thick, black smoke or hissing steam. Its days of usefulness were long since over. It now rested like a faithful old workhorse on a sidetrack where it browsed in contentment and scorned the smooth, flashy brightness of the new diesel engines. The old steam engine was not neglected for it still shone and gleamed from the devoted ministrations of countless willing hands, which ensured its existence in a world dominated by the silent sleekness of the diesel trains. It was content to remain a living museum and paid no heed to the smokeless conceit of the new trains, muted except for an ugly nasal blast and without character or personality. The old engine was unmoved by the bustle that was going on about it and barely acknowledged the glances of wonderment and incredulity from those who paused to admire its obsolete grandeur. It had seen much service in many parts of the country but it was now left to the new race of metal giants to perform such tasks.

Such a metal giant was even now waiting to perform its

appointed task. The night train from Leningrad to Moscow would travel some seven hundred kilometres and was scheduled to stop only once, at Kalinin. Already it was close to departure time and the carriages, and compartments within the carriages, were filling up although there would still be plenty of room for the last minute passengers, providing they did not mind forfeiting a sleeping berth. Most of the compartments housed bunks for four persons but if not in use then up to twice as many could be accommodated. The sensible Russian always made use of the sleeping berths. Not all Russians, however, were sensible - or maybe there were other reasons why the sleeping berths in the last compartment of the last carriage would not be used.

It was almost time, and as the large hand of the station clock jerked its way towards the hour, only a few passengers were lingering on the platform. These were mainly the tourists who were still trying to sort out their luggage from the untidy piles into which the mountain had now disintegrated. The tourists, mainly the schoolchildren, still retained a sense of order despite the growing urgency, perhaps because they were more adaptable and co-operative than adults, whose inherent sense of possession would have sent them scrambling among the luggage to recover their own personal suitcase. Of course Russian children would have been even better organised.

Most of the tourists occupied the last two carriages with the exception of the very last compartment. This particular compartment might have been specially reserved though there was nothing to indicate this. In any event it was the only one at the rear of the train, which had not yet been filled.

The conductress waited on the platform as the last passengers boarded her train, before taking her place in the last carriage. Her expression betrayed neither anxiety nor exasperation with these few latecomers. It remained perpetually sour and forbidding. She was only concerned with the prompt departure of the night train and when it was time she would signal through to the driver. Her own quarters were next to the last compartment. They were functional rather than comfortable but, unlike the old time guards van, hers was an office and a control centre, with buttons, knobs, dials and a multitude of technological gadgetry to assist her in the running of the train.

It was almost time for departure. The conductress squinted along the platform and then looked back to the barrier. There appeared to be no latecomers so she climbed aboard. To those inside the train the slamming of doors was the only signal that departure was imminent.

The last compartment was now filled to its normal capacity, which in a sleeper is for four people. There were now four people in that compartment - four adults that is, for one was a young woman with a baby. The most striking of these passengers was undoubtedly the tall, attractive woman of about thirty-five who seemed oddly out of place. Her bright golden hair was mostly concealed beneath an expensive fur hat but her sharp blue eyes shone with an alert intelligence as she glanced at her fellow passengers and quickly took in all the details of the compartment. Having seen all she wanted she leaned against the padded seat and closed her eyes. Her name was Irina...Y - just Irina. It is perhaps better not to know too much about this lady. She was Russian and like many Russians she possessed a secret, which for the moment she wished not to disclose. Her reasons were her own and certainly no business of the other passengers. Most Russians, however, were quite happy to mind their own business.

Unlike the golden haired, stately Irina, the other passengers were much more ordinary, to look at that is. However, what lay beneath their ordinary exteriors may be something altogether different.

Before the train had begun to move on its long journey the four passengers, five with the small baby, were already seated. In one corner was a fearsome looking woman of indeterminate age. She looked as typical a Russian as the attractive Irina did not. She had a sort of solid, square face, with small inquisitive eyes and a jutting jaw, which seemed to be permanently clamped. Her clothes were cheap and drab, almost deliberately so, but somehow conveyed an air of self-indulgence in the way she wore them. She was not all that she seemed to be. As she entered the compartment she looked at nothing but the empty window seat and made straight for it. She paused only to nudge her own stubby foot against the smart boots of Irina. She could have got past without any difficulty and without disturbing anybody, but she wanted to make a point. She was as good as anybody else and all comrades were equal.

The attractive Irina made no comment but moved her foot just enough to allow her to pass.

Olga Dubretskova plopped into the corner seat as one who had successfully conquered that small space and was determined to hold it against all comers. She gently placed the small, bulky bag she had been hugging to her chest, on the floor between her feet. With only the briefest of glances at her fellow passengers she turned to the window and stared hard at the station outside.

Of the other two passengers, neither seemed disposed or inclined to contest the other corner seat, not when they had to sit facing the redoubtable, square faced Olga. The young woman, clutching a baby, was seated near the corridor and opposite to a young man who looked like a student. The young woman was nervous, or at least she appeared to be. Her entrance into the compartment was fraught with anxiety at having to sit with other people. Her large brown eyes were constantly flickering from one passenger to another trying to decide which one she feared the least. It was not clear why she should fear any of them but then that may not have been her usual manner. When she eventually sat down, it was on the edge of the seat and as far away from the others as she could manage. The child in her arms seemed content for it made no protest at the constant shuffling of the young mother. The woman's name was Natalia. There was no other name to go with it, not any longer. Whenever a second name was required she used the name Valinska, as shown on her papers. It was not her real name. Her real name was hidden behind those nervous eyes. She was young, not much above twenty and might perhaps be regarded as pretty but she was thin and her skin had an unhealthy, sallow appearance. She looked as though she had been neglecting herself or had been neglected by someone. Her clothes were ordinary, mostly cheap stuff, but she was well kept and tidy. The attractive, blond-haired woman had smiled at her but her nervousness was not abated. She had tried to smile in return but the smile would not come.

Almost opposite the young woman with the child, and on the same seat as the attractive Irina, sat the young man. He was a student and, like many of the young Russians today, managed to display an aggressive arrogance in the way he dressed. Despite the temperature outside he had refrained from doing up the buttons of his coat or his shirt, which was open at the neck. His trousers were a cheap imitation of the more durable western type of denim, while he spurned good sensible boots in favour of a pair of light training shoes. They were good enough but they couldn't withstand the heavy snows. He projected, or tried to project, an image of untidiness, which in turn was supposed to proclaim his own personal defiance at the system. He was almost a rebel. His clean-shaven features and neat, correct hairstyle, however, betrayed his conformity.

He hardly looked at anyone else, not even the attractive woman next to him. He was much more concerned with portraying his own image than taking notice of his fellow passengers. His name was Mikhail. He had another name but he rarely used it preferring to keep his identity as much of a secret as possible.

As the compartment was a sleeper all four passengers could have taken the opportunity to make use of the bunks. The conductress had already proclaimed, in a loud voice, how the upper berths could be swung down and fastened into place. Everyone had listened but no one had taken any notice. In fact, apart from a few glances nobody had spoken.

In the corridor of the coach the conductress was marching along checking that all doors were closed and all windows fastened. She was also looking to see that everything was in order and no one was breaking the rules - her rules.

As with most trains prior to departure, the corridor was crowded with people taking a last look at the station or waving to friends and relations. In this coach the people were all tourists, French or English - the conductress couldn't tell which. She scowled as she spotted that one of the younger tourists had succeeded in opening one of the non-opening windows. Such a thing was expressly forbidden and she tried to convey as much. With a sharp flick of her wrist she snapped it shut, much to the consternation of the adult in charge of the children, who had been struggling with both hands to force its closure. Her action had caused some amusement among the tourists as one of them made a quick comparison of muscular strength between the two of them. She appreciated the joke and her toothy smile joined them in a genuine show of mirth. But her humour was strictly reserved for the foreigners, for upon catching sight of the young student poking his head out of the last compartment she barked at him. "The train is about to move. No getting off now!"

Totally abashed the student quickly slid the connecting door closed and sank back in his seat. He had heard the laughter so naturally he was curious. The others in the compartment were also interested and each of them would have liked to know the reason for such explosions of mirth, especially if the grim-faced conductress was involved. But they could bear not knowing.

The student was at first a little red-faced from the rebuke, now grinned slightly to himself. It was worth it just to hear the laughter.

Whatever thoughts or conjectures these four passengers in the last compartment may have entertained, they were soon replaced with a new sensation, for at last the train began to move. There had been no discernible warning, like the shriek of a whistle or a blast of steam. Not like the old days! Somewhere up ahead there may have been a muffled snort of the new diesel's claxon but nothing else.

There was hardly a rumble as the carriages began to glide

slowly out of the station. The night train from Leningrad had begun its journey.

Chapter Two
Irina

Irina... her other name is best not mentioned, always felt that a train journey, or any kind of journey really, had never properly begun till she was finally planted in the seat of her particular transport. She had no qualms about the train not starting on time or anything like that. Russian trains were efficient and always on time. She leaned back and rested her head against the upholstery behind her and half closed her eyes.

For many people, and her colleagues were numbered among them, she was a puzzle. She was not exactly young but still very much in the full flower of womanhood. Her figure was feminine and curved most attractively in the right places. There was no misshapen bulkiness about her, despite the heavy, expensive fur coat and those smart boots. Her elegance was clearly defined and anywhere else would no doubt have evoked some sort of comment from her fellow passengers; appraisal from the men and envy from the women. She was not so much a mystery in herself but there was something faintly mysterious, perhaps with a tiny hint of menace, about her. Her gait, her carriage, and her general demeanour gave nothing away. She might have been a star athlete, or a dancer from the Kirov, but she was just a little too old for those occupations, so much the preserve of the young and very young. Her face was made up but only enough to enhance her own sharply delineated beauty. High cheekbones and a clear, tanned skin might have belonged to a Hollywood film star, but her keen blue eyes were much too intelligent and much too alert. She was a beautiful woman at the height of her powers and, by Russian standards, one who appeared to be quite wealthy. What then was she doing travelling alone, in the dead of night, on this train, and in this compartment?

Irina smiled to herself, partly because of the secret she held but mostly because she was remembering.

'"Oh to be in England now that April's here". That's what he would have said. I smile to myself at the thought. How odd I should think of such a thing. Yet it is April, and I am certainly not in England. In all honesty I can't say that I particularly want to be in England - at least - not at this precise moment. I smile to myself again, this time at the idea of me wanting something so extraordinary. I lean back in my seat and contemplate my fellow passengers. There are only three of them so far but I feel sure that the compartment will fill up before long. We are due to leave at 11p.m. For some strange reason I have a sudden fear that we may not leave on time. But the night train from Leningrad is never late. Maybe I am a little nervous or over anxious. I try to close my eyes, but it is no good. I can only sleep while the train is moving.'

"Excuse me!"

'A woman, square and bulky, pushed at my feet with a sharp prod of her unfeminine boot to indicate that she wanted to get past me. There is plenty of room. I do not stretch my legs out like some people but she probably wanted to make a point. Her look was not entirely unfriendly yet neither did she smile. 'We are all comrades together', I could imagine her saying. I have to agree though, for in this compartment of this train we certainly are, and for the next eight hours or so at least. The thought doesn't trouble me too much. I have put up with people like her all my life. There now - she is happy, with her square bulk squeezed into the corner and her square face pressed against the window. Once out of the station, she won't be able to see much for already it is quite dark. At the moment the station, with its lights, provides an illusion of brightness, but it will disappear once we have slid out from its protective canopy. There may be just a little light for there is still plenty of snow about, left over from the winter, and that always makes it seem brighter. I wonder if we might after all have the sleeper to ourselves. If so that would mean that we are full with just the four of us. It is difficult to tell with the authorities. They may just decide to put more people in here. I don't mind. I can never really sleep on a train anyway - leastways not in one of those cots. I can quite contentedly doze while seated. At the moment the beds are neatly tucked out of sight. In fact so cleverly had they been constructed within the framework of the compartment that it is difficult to tell that it is a sleeper at all. As I think about this my eyes begin to wander about the compartment looking for the telltale latches and clips. The square faced woman suddenly takes an interest and her eyes follow mine.'

"Not a sleeper," she grunts in a satisfied monotone and she goes back to her window.

'Well that explains her eagerness to get a window seat. There are no bunks to get in the way.

Still fifteen minutes to go. I look at the other two passengers. One is a young woman with a small baby. She looks unhappy and ill at ease. Maybe it is her first experience of travelling by train. It could be, for many people from the outlying villages around Leningrad hardly ever moved from the one place in a whole lifetime. They're better off I would say. The big cities have nothing much to offer them. I had smiled at the girl when she entered but she could only manage a nervous twitch of the mouth in response. The baby, by its bulk, must be about six months old I should think. It was asleep in her arms. I like children but I can only hope that it will remain that way for the better part of the journey. The young woman is sitting uncomfortably on the edge of the seat. She is still nervous, perhaps even afraid. It is difficult to tell with some women. So many things can affect them. Not like square face in the corner. She is obviously well past being affected. But this young woman is definitely afraid. Where is her husband? I always try to assume the best about people, especially Russian people. Is she going to meet him? Has she left him behind? Running away from him perhaps. So many possibilities and the only way to find out is to ask her. I can't do that. I can only smile at her. This time it produces a sickly suspicion of a smile in return. Well, that is something I suppose. The other occupant is a man. He looks interesting. He too is youngish and like the young he dresses quite casually and deliberately untidily. He is clean-shaven though and has a neat haircut, which seems at variance with the manner in which he is dressed. I can sense a rebellious spirit beneath his calm exterior. His manner of dress defies all the old values. He wants to be different but I can tell that it is more than that. He wants to proclaim that difference - shout it to the world. His world has forbidden such unseemly and unpatriotic outbursts. There is no individuality of life here in Russia. He is probably no different from many young men who feel some inner compulsion to establish their place and make their own special mark on the world. Young men have thoughts like that. But such thoughts are soon withered in the Siberian snows. It is a pity in a way. I cannot resist smiling inwardly at my own sense of superiority. I can afford to be generous, even though my thoughts sometimes border on the treasonable. I know about such men, whose passions are all the ambition they need, like my father when he was a young man. Not today. All that is long over. The Revolution had need of such passions, then. No longer. We have learned the harsh realities and have ever since kept our passions in check. If we had not done so they would have done for us. Suddenly I feel a great sorrow for the young man sitting next to me and yet it gives me a warm pleasure to look at him. He reminds me so much of that Englishman, a younger version maybe. That's probably why I smiled at him I suppose, though he didn't react much to my smile. Even if I am a Russian, I am still a woman and I like to think that my smile has some merit. My Englishman taught me that. This young man was a Russian, no doubt of it. I could see the smile behind his eyes longing to get out but fear and suspicion kept it hidden. I don't blame him really. Not like my Englishman. Why 'my' Englishman? I should not have thought that for I can feel myself blushing. Of course he is my Englishman. "Oh to be in England..." He used to say that to tease me I think. I loved his teasing, as I loved him. He would have smiled at any pretty young woman. 'A smile is a tribute to beauty', he used to say whenever I caught him smiling at other women. I used to laugh at the boyish exuberance he would display and yet at the same time envied his freedom of spirit. I still envy that. He taught me that some things are beyond the restrictions of culture, race, religion and most of all politics. I never argued with him. He is not Russian. He can never know or understand how such ordinary things, like smiling, have been purchased at a great price. I never said anything to him but I loved him and I loved the spirit that shone from him. For a Russian it is a dangerous thing to have such a spirit. The young man next to me knows that very well. That is why he did not smile. He doesn't trust me. He doesn't trust anyone he doesn't know well. And he is right - more than perhaps he realises. Can he be trusted, I wonder?

I must stop thinking about that Englishman. I long for him to be here with me on this train. I long to feel him close so that he could again persuade me that life is indeed full of beautiful things. I will cry if I think about him any more because I know that I do not deserve to have him here. I have cheated him. He doesn't know it and will probably never know. Had we been in another world - another country perhaps, I too could have experienced some of that freedom. I could then tell him the truth. He might have smiled at me or even teased me and I would have laughed and cried together with a new kind of happiness. There is still time for me to go back and tell him.

Alas, it is too late. Silently, smoothly, almost imperceptibly, the train begins to move. I heave a deep sigh and look quickly with a sudden alarm at my fellow passengers to see if they have noticed. No. They are much too interested in themselves.'

"About time we moved."

'The square faced woman in the corner of the

compartment spoke, without turning her head, as if she were addressing her own reflection in the window. I take a quick, surreptitious look at my watch. Eleven p.m. - on time as usual. I look across at her and hope that during the course of the journey her remarks, inaccurate though they may be, will be few and brief as already. For some reason she irritates me and without cause I find myself disliking her presence. Perhaps there is something in that brusqueness of manner of hers, which is reminiscent of those earlier days. She looks like an informer. But even such people have their part to play.

As the train glides out of the station it seems suddenly to become much brighter. In reality of course it is still dark but once away from the station and out into the open, patches of snow will become more evident. There is a noise in the corridor. It sounds like a quarrel - or was it laughter? No doubt the conductress will deal with it without any assistance. She is another square faced Russian who will do what is necessary to preserve the smooth running of the train, short of actual physical violence - I think. The young student slides back the door to find out the cause of the noise and all he gets for his trouble is the sharp edge of her tongue. Red-faced he quickly slides the door shut and sinks back into his seat.

I look around at my companions once again, especially the young woman with the baby. She has relaxed a little now that the train is moving - not very fast at the moment, but any movement seems to satisfy her. She still cannot smile and almost cowers back against the seat. Why is she so afraid and so nervous? Why be afraid of me? I can't resist chuckling to myself at that thought. It is the irony of the situation I suppose. I cannot help thinking about the irony of so many things. It is that Englishman's fault. He can always see the funny side of things. That's what he told me I must do. So I am doing it. Seeing the funny side of things. But it doesn't make me laugh and it doesn't comfort me. I look at the young woman again and try to convey as much disinterest in my glance as possible. It is a waste of time. She isn't looking. She doesn't seem to be very strong. But looks can be deceptive. I can only hope so.

The train is gathering speed. I glance out of the window and see the thousand pinpoints of light spread out in the darkness like a twinkling carpet. I never realised that Leningrad was so big. Cities always seems much larger at night. It is the lights I suppose. They have a habit of disguising distance. Now there is more snow and fewer lights. We will soon be on the outskirts of the city. The train has picked up speed and I can feel the gradual surge of power. It will soon build up its own rhythmic pattern, which no doubt will help to send us to sleep. I don't feel like sleeping. Too much to think about and too much time in which to think. Then there are my companions, four of them - with the baby.

The train is now moving quite fast. We have passed the outskirts of Leningrad and are now out in the country. There is still not much to see out of the windows except the occasional white patch of snow. There are a lot of trees, which grow in profusion as we move further away from the city. The snow is only visible in the clearings between these great swathes of trees. It is the end of winter but with the temperature hovering around zero it takes a long time for the snow to disappear out here in the countryside. I am not really looking out of the window but it is better than looking at the faces of my companions. I sigh inwardly. What a dreary bunch they are. Are all Russians like them I wonder? I close my eyes and pretend that I am somewhere else, back in Leningrad in my apartment. There I would by now be in bed and snuggled up to my warm Englishman. It is so easy to fall into the luxury provided by my imagination. Our lovemaking has always been a beautiful thing and it is not difficult to recapture those precious moments and linger there in undiluted pleasure. There were never any conditions to our love. My Englishman was either too shrewd or too innocent to probe beyond the surface of my life. For my own part I am more than grateful that he loved me for being a woman and nothing more. I am glad of that. I will always be glad that I had such a man. If life were only different, if I could have told him if... if, but maybe I would have frightened him away. I don't know about Englishmen. I know that a Russian man would have been frightened away. I do not want to dream of such things. I only want to get back to him, where I know that I will be warm and safe - and satisfied. Neither of us would look for answers nor worry about the future. We would be content just to be together.

I dream on and am beginning to become drowsy.

How far we have travelled I have no idea. I steal another look at my wristwatch - eleven forty-five. Still a long way to go but I don't mind too much. The compartment is warm and the others are silent. I am glad of that for I don't want them bursting into my thoughts with useless chatter. People will always chatter at the wrong times and usually think that they are doing you a good turn by dragging you into their insipid conversations. Though I am not exactly sleeping I close my eyes. If I pretend then perhaps I will be left alone.'

"That's a nice watch."

'I open my eyes with a start and find the square faced woman looking directly at me. She nods towards my wrist.'

"Where did you get it?"

'She enquires imperiously, her small eyes screwing up almost into pinpoints. Her inquisitiveness is overpowering and well matches her rudeness.

I am sure that I had blushed slightly but I try to sound casual in my reply.'

"A present."

'The square faced woman leans forward slightly and looks me straight in the eye, her bulldog face glowering with dislike and distrust.'

"I bet. For services rendered more like - in bed."

'With that she sank back and regards me as a culprit caught out in a lie.

I can do little except to say no and give her an icy stare, from which she eventually breaks away and turns once more to her vigil at the window.

I feel annoyed and irritated. However, I reason that it is my own fault for choosing to travel this way. I had chosen anonymity so I must put up with such things.

The young student suddenly shows some interest in the remarks of the square faced woman and looks at me with a new regard. It seems as though he is on the point of smiling but my own look freezes the smile out of him.

I could curse that woman, not because of her rudeness and innuendo but because she is typical of a certain type of person. No doubt she is greedy. She has that greedy look about her and she begrudges anyone having the temerity to own anything like a wristwatch, which I can plainly see she covets with all of her podgy heart. I suppose she is a good Russian and probably believes in the system but, like many others, her communism only works if she gets her fair share and more besides. 'Take from the rich and those that have, and give to me', is her motto I daresay. I try to ignore her presence and concentrate on something else. I can only hope that she will keep quiet for the rest of the journey though I am sure that I will be disappointed.

The train rumbles on into the night and once more the gentle vibrations of wheels over tracks begin to produce the inevitable soporific effect and I feel myself becoming drowsy once more. I can hardly keep my eyes open and yet I don't really feel tired. I am soon back in the arms of my Englishman. In a way, old square face in the corner is right. My wristwatch was a present - from my Englishman. It had been a parting gift. My parting gift to him had been a promise that I would return soon. I will not return. How could I tell him such a thing? My life is not my own. Already I have taken risks. In my heart I know I would always have to take such risks for the joy and happiness I discovered in Leningrad. Now I am travelling back to reality and only while I am on this train can I indulge in a few more hours of luxury in thinking about those times. This train is like a no-mans land, a limbo in between worlds. When it reaches Moscow then my parting from him will be complete. No more shall I think of him and he must not think of me. As the finality of our parting begins to grip me I suddenly realise that he might easily come to Moscow to find me. Why should he? He will forget me soon enough. Even so I cannot help wondering if he will come. I like to think that he will care enough for me to want to come. It pleases my vanity I suppose. At the same time I know that he mustn't. He would only find disappointment and perhaps danger if we met again. In any case it is not very likely. On reflection perhaps it is just as well that I am travelling back to Moscow this way. These few hours will give me time to sort out my feelings and prepare for what lies ahead of me. I feel sad and strangely, with every passing mile, I grow sadder.

Suddenly I am conscious of being scrutinised. I open my eyes and find the square faced woman staring at me. In fact they are all staring at me, even the nervous young woman. What can it mean? Then I realise. Without thinking I have been letting my emotions get the better of me and I had begun to weep, not heavily but enough to attract their attention. Russians are a naturally inquisitive race and they will fasten onto any small peculiarity but will say nothing. I am too surprised at myself to feel embarrassed but, nevertheless, I have the presence of mind to quickly reach for a handkerchief and affect a sneeze. Mild curiosity is one thing but I don't want to become the object of their scrutiny. The three of them say nothing. I think I have successfully convinced them of an approaching cold for they soon begin to turn back to their own thoughts, that is if they had any thoughts. For myself I am determined to keep a tight grip on my emotions. It is surprising how one can be fooled. I wondered how I might have reacted had I taken a plane. Perhaps after all I'm better off for this longer journey. I stare out of the window and see nothing but an occasional ribbon of snow reflected in the darkness. There would be more snow visible if it were not for the trees. Having travelled this journey before I know that we are passing through areas of forest and the darkness is due to the tall pines keeping out the snow. Sometimes lighter patches indicate clumps of silver birch. There is no longer any sign of habitation, though it would be near impossible to tell even if there was. The lamp of a farmer's cottage would have to shine bright to pierce the opaque pine. There is nothing to see out there except shades of blackness.

I want to return to my Englishman, in my thoughts, but I do not want to experience another embarrassing outbreak of tears. I continue to sniff into my handkerchief in order to keep up the pretence of an approaching cold. The others, however, no longer seem to be interested. Perhaps I really want to go back to him - back to Leningrad. I could be making a mistake in leaving him without any explanation. I should have told him the truth but I was afraid that I would lose him. How silly. I have lost him anyway. I can't turn the train around - though I could get off at Kalinin. What nonsense. I have a job in Moscow - an important job. That must come before any private feelings. Such things must always come second to the job and of course - the Party. I sigh, a small sigh to myself, and try to come to terms with the situation. After all it is my own fault for taking a holiday to see my parents in Leningrad. How was I to know that I would meet Harry? Perhaps I ought to have taken a holiday earlier.

I look out of the window again and wonder how far we have travelled. I almost look at my watch but think better of it. I don't want square face making further remarks. Instead I just lean back and close my eyes. As soon as I do then there is the sound of raised voices in the corridor. We all look towards the door and the student is about to lean forward and open it but then he remembers his earlier scolding from the conductress and decides against it. From the tone it sounds like an argument and the conductress is involved. Whether she is protecting her passengers from some unruly element among the tourists further down the corridor, or is being her usual awkward self, I cannot tell. I don't really care. I am beginning to wish that this journey would come to an end. I have made up my mind about one thing. I will definitely fly next time. Will there be a next time?

My opportunity to lapse into conjecture quickly evaporates as suddenly the door of the compartment is slid back with a harsh rasping sound as the castors swished violently along the guiding rail, till I thought that the door would slide straight through to the next compartment. Framed in the doorway, in the gloom, for the lights on the train provided only sufficient illumination to prevent one stumbling in the dark, was the solid figure of the conductress. She glares balefully at each of us in turn, like an angry teacher who suspects her pupils of some misdemeanour and has just failed to catch them in the act. She says nothing and just grunts. I can't tell whether it is a grunt of satisfaction or not. In any event it doesn't matter for from the gloom she suddenly produces a squirming figure of a man. In the poor light it looks as though she is holding him by the scruff of the neck. But it is not the case. As soon as the man himself materialised, then there, behind him, is a much larger figure of another man. This other man, with his dark, early Chicago type hat and imitation leather coat, pushes the smaller man before him. The smaller man, already cowering, cannot help but stumble over one of the passengers, the young man I think, for he is next to the door. His stumble causes him to fall into the compartment and land at the feet of the young woman. She gives a short, frightened squeal and edges back in her seat. If she could have stood on it I'm sure she would have done so.

The man struggles to his knees and gives a sad smile to the young woman.'

"I…I beg your pardon. I am so clumsy."

'The young woman gives a slight gasp and points to his face.'

"You're bleeding."

'She speaks in a strange sort of voice, as though she is about to break out into a hysterical laugh. I hope not. She doesn't. Instead she just cradles her baby closer and continues to stare at the man as he struggles to his feet.

The big man turns to the conductress and mutters something. Though I cannot hear what he says it seems that it doesn't please her. I know how she feels. It is her train and she doesn't like people telling her what to do even if they are secret policemen.

The fact that this big man is obviously a member of the secret police doesn't deter the square faced woman in the corner from muttering and grumbling, as he forced the smaller man onto the same seat and squashes himself beside him.'

"This is for four. No room for anyone else."

'The square faced woman grunts and shuffles on her seat to emphasise this statement.

The big man just looks at her stonily. With another shuffle and another grunt she turns back to the window.

The policeman, for I have no doubt that's what he is, then looks at each of us in turn. Both the young student and the girl with the baby try to avoid his stare. It seems that they also recognise a secret policeman when they see one. But he looks at them as though they are beneath his consideration. I know that look.

He then looks at me and I return his stare. Whether he thinks that I am using some sort of feminine charm on him I can't imagine, but for a brief moment he allows his grim, ugly features to break into a smile. It is hardly that. He has obviously never been used to smiling in an open way. His thick lips part slightly showing uneven yellow teeth, and his eyes look at me in a kind of furtive manner, almost as if he is leering at a suspect, and not a very attractive suspect at that. I feel insulted and want to speak but I remember where I am and am suddenly very conscious of my own secret. I stare hard at him and for a second I see a flicker of uncertainty - not quite fear - a doubt maybe. He feels that he might have misinterpreted my look. For that brief moment he was uncomfortable for he had made a misjudgement. I am glad of his discomfiture.

The presence of this black-coated policeman does nothing to improve the atmosphere though I don't suppose he really makes that much difference. None of the others have seemed inclined to speak or show any kind of life before he had burst in amongst us anyway. In a strange sort of way I am glad of his presence, loathsome though it is, because it keeps me from thinking too much about other things. As I look at those heavy, leering features, I can see more clearly that I am doing the right thing. Alas no more Leningrad and no more of my Englishman.'

Chapter Three
Olga

Olga, the square faced woman, allowed her thin-lipped face to break into a smile. The others in the compartment couldn't see her smile nor would she have wished them to. She peered intently out of the window from her corner seat and stared hard at the goings on in the station. She couldn't see that much but she liked to be looking at things - and people. Her small round eyes hardly seemed to swivel in their sockets but nevertheless they were still able to see everything in front of her. She was not plump but her figure was almost matching her face in its squareness. Her shape was totally unfeminine and she did not attempt to disguise it. In many ways she might have been mistaken for a typical Russian peasant, but her pasty complexion and shiftiness in her manner was more than ample evidence that she was a city dweller who was concerned only in getting what she could for herself. She was not married, at least not now, and it is difficult to imagine such a face and form ever entering into any contract, which might involve a degree of emotion or intimacy. The only one Olga loved, or had ever loved, was herself. In age she was probably not much older than the attractive Irina, who sat almost opposite her. The fact that they were both in the same compartment on the night train from Leningrad, however, was the only thing they had in common, that and a secret they shared. Olga was not bothered. She despised those who had more than she, especially if they openly flaunted themselves or their wealth. She was a true daughter of the system. She knew her limitations and would never stoop to prostitution, though she had considered it. To Olga life was series of battles and skirmishes, like getting the corner seat in a railway compartment. She smiled again and relived the small triumph in her mind.

'They all wanted this seat but I got it. What do you think of that you painted tart? I'll bet that's what she is. Nothing but a whore, or where else did she get those clothes and that wristwatch. She tries to hide it but I saw it. The others don't look up to much either. That young chap in the corner looks fishy. I bet he's a student. Can tell that by his clothes. He'd better be keeping his fancy opinions to himself. I know what these students are like. It's a wonder that he and that tart haven't got together. He's got no money I suppose, least not enough for her. I've seen her smiling at him. Well, she'll be disappointed there. Pity it's so dark. I like looking out of the window. That way I can keep an eye on everything that goes on inside as well as out there. Yes, I like a corner seat next to a window. I wonder if I'll be able to stay awake. I aim to because I don't trust this lot. That young one with the baby looks odd. That child of hers hasn't made a sound since she got on this train. I never knew a baby to be so quiet. Sickly I suppose. The mother doesn't look much better - half starved. She's a queer one all right. Where's her husband I wonder? I bet she isn't married. Just like these young ones of today. No morals. No, she certainly doesn't look too good. If she had a husband he'd be with her. That's where a husband should be, at his wife's side. I wonder what happened to my old man? Now there was a husband. What a waste of time he was. I'm better off without him, I know that much. Him and his family! They never liked me. It was those sisters of his. I could hate them but why bother. They did me a good turn taking him back to his precious mother. I'm definitely better off without him. Good riddance! Anyway he had some very funny friends. I shouldn't be surprised if he was mixed up in something illegal. If he were in trouble, the police would have got him by now. He was too stupid to be crooked. Good riddance again! I wouldn't be travelling on this train to Moscow if I'd still been tied to him. Proper stick-in-the-mud he was. I'm looking forward to Moscow. I could do a lot of good for myself there. Leningrad was all right but too slow. Besides, it was getting dangerous. Moscow will be different. That Gum store sounds just the place. I should do plenty of business there. It's always crowded like Gostinny Dvor I hear. I hope that Josef hasn't forgotten to meet me. It'll be all right. I can rely on him. He'll have everything set up and waiting. I don't have to worry. I can sit back and relax and maybe catch an hour or two of sleep. No one will be able to touch my bag without waking me. I'll just pretend for a while and see if anyone tries to be nosey. I know what these Leningraders are like. I should do. I've lived among them all my life. I bet it's the same in Moscow. Big cities are always the same - no conscience. Governments don't have any so why should we, the people. There are too many people in the Party. Good job I keep myself to myself. I'll not get rich in the Party. But I suppose it has it uses, though what they are I can't guess. My husband - my ex husband now, he was a Party member, and served on committees for this and that. Never did him any good. Never made him rich. The fool. He didn't even use the opportunities, which were under his nose. Just think how much he could have found out about people, neighbours or even family. I should like to have found out something about those sisters of his. Oh yes I would have loved to get some dirt on them. They would have sung a different tune if I had got my way with them. Too suspicious they were. I bet they were on the game, just like that one over there. They were not so lucky though. Never had much money or fine clothes. Still they were his sisters so it's hardly surprising. And that old mother of his - what a dragon she was. How could I have been so stupid in the first place? Anyway, that's all gone now - thank goodness. Looking forward to Moscow. I just want nothing to go wrong to spoil it for me.

I think I will lean back and doze for a while. I can't see anything from the window any more. All the light has gone and it's almost black out there. There are still some patches of snow, which flash past like waving flags. Not much to look at though. At least I can still see the reflection of the others. If I twist round into the corner perhaps I can still keep an eye on them without too much trouble. I wonder how long we've been travelling. That's one thing I'm going to get when I'm in Moscow, a good wristwatch. That woman on the opposite seat has got one. I saw it, although she tries to hide it. I wonder how she came by it, though I bet I can guess. There – she's looking at it now. I can ask her.

"Nice watch," I say pleasantly. "Where did you get it?"

'A present,' she replies and goes red. That's a sure sign of a guilty conscience.

"I bet. For services rendered - in bed."

I can see the look on her face as I mention that. It had hit hard I could tell. She didn't deny it although she gives me a look that could kill. Strange though, I believe that she would kill if she thought she had reason enough. She's got that look about her. Not like the usual tart. I don't trust her, whatever sort of whore she is. I don't trust any of them.

I look at the others again as casually as I can. I haven't really paid them much notice. That young woman is still holding her brat as if she expects someone to snatch it away from her. I'd love to know whether she's married or not. Why is she going to Moscow? To get away from him I shouldn't wonder. I don't blame her for that. Men are pigs. If she isn't married then why bother. Going back to mother I suppose, with an extra bundle. It's the quietest baby I ever came across. Still I mustn't complain. It makes for a quiet time and there's still a good way to go I should think.

I lean back and close my eyes or rather half close them, and just hope that the journey will be over quickly. I suppose that I am tired but I don't really want to go to sleep. I wish I could keep a check on my bag. I ought to look inside and see that everything's all right. I daren't do it here, in this compartment.

I don't know why I should worry. I've checked it a hundred times already. It's all there. Yes, I'm looking forward to Moscow and those shops.

I might have fallen asleep. I couldn't tell but suddenly I am wide-awake. Something must have disturbed me. I can see that young student poke his head out into the corridor. I think I heard laughing or a row of some sort. He soon pulls his head back. Nearly bitten off by that conductress I daresay. I am not surprised there. Typical of officials, puffed up with their own importance. That young man won't do that again in a hurry. I bet she wouldn't have shouted at me like that. I wouldn't have given her a chance. She'd soon get a mouthful. Anyway she hasn't got any right to treat passengers like cattle. All that went out years ago. She must think that Comrade Stalin is still the boss. Stalin - now there was a man. Not that I'd fancy him in my bed. Anyway I've had enough of men. They're all weak and spineless. If there's dirty work to be done you can bet it'll be given to a woman first.

I look across at that student. He seems as though he has lost some of his cockiness. He's like all the younger generation. They do a lot of shouting but that's about all. He's the same. Tries to pretend he's a big man but underneath he's nothing. Look at him now. All the stuffing knocked out of him, just because a conductress on a train shouted at him. He could have shouted back. That's what you have to do with these jumped up officials - shout at them. If that doesn't work then show them the Party card. That always shuts then up. They're never quite sure after that.

The time is beginning to drag though I don't suppose we've been travelling for more than half an hour, and there's nothing to see out of the window. What a boring journey. I could do with a drink. Good job I brought some vodka along though I don't fancy taking a drink here, not with this lot. I'll slip off to the lavatory in a minute. The train is running smooth and I can hear only a slight clatter of the wheels. I can feel myself nodding off again. I'll make sure that my bag is secure between my feet.

Whether I had slept for long I can't tell but suddenly I am wide awake. My first thought is my bag. It is still there between my feet undisturbed. What had woken me up was a noise in the corridor. It is still there and sounds like an argument. The conductress is one of them. I can tell her voice. I see the student about to grab the door and see what is happening but then he thinks better of it. The row lasts for only a minute or so then it stops. Suddenly the door of our compartment is slung back and there is the conductress. She looks in a right state. She is worked up about something, I can tell. I thought for a minute she was going to say something to us. I remember my vodka bottle. But she just looks around and grunts. Before any of us can work out what she wants a man suddenly appears in the doorway. It looks as though she has dragged him out of the corridor by the scruff of his neck. But I am wrong. She might be a tough old bird but she can't be that strong. As soon as this weed of a man steps into the compartment I can see that another much bigger man is holding him. It is gloomy in the corridor so I can't see much of him. He is big and strong because he pushes this other chap into our compartment with such a force that he stumbles over that young student. He falls at the feet of that woman with the child. I nearly smile as she almost lets out a squeal and squeezes back onto her seat. But it is no laughing matter. We already have our share in this compartment, especially as it is a sleeper. I'll tell him so.

"Only four to this compartment. No room for anyone else."

The big chap doesn't say anything. He just looks at me as if I was dirt. I don't like the look of him either. Now he is in our compartment I can see that he isn't one of the world's beauties. He doesn't have to be of course. He is a secret policeman. I know that right enough. I've seen his kind before but it doesn't mean he has the right to push in and sit down on my seat with that squint of a man next to me. His prisoner I suppose. Well - I don't fancy either of them. If they keep to themselves for the rest of the journey I can put up with it. I don't want any trouble now I've got this far. Anyway, that fancy piece had better behave herself. I noticed that the policeman has been looking at her. Odd though, how she looked at him. I wonder about her. She doesn't seem scared of him. Not like that poor thing at the other end of the seat. If she squeezes back any more she'll be out in the corridor. She is scared all right. Can't say I blame her though. I'd be scared in her place. What - with a baby and no husband! Not that a man would be much use against his sort. I know what they're like. Shoot you as soon as look at you, and other things. I'm only surprised that he bothered to bring a prisoner with him. He must be pretty important. I can smell trouble. Why couldn't he have picked another carriage? And why did he take so long in picking this one? He must have got on at Leningrad. I don't suppose anyone else would put up with him. The tourists! That's it! Can't upset them. That's why he's in with us.

I look at him again. Dressed in black, even black gloves. They're all the same. They seem to take a pride in being stupid. Do they really think that by dressing like that they become like other people. Maybe he thinks he's invisible. More like he doesn't care. Look at that face. I thought my husband was pretty poor for looks - but this one! Well at least it suits his trade. That other one looks harmless enough, more like a beggar. I can't see him full face without turning round and facing him and I don't want to do that. I mustn't attract too much attention to myself. He must be important yet he doesn't seem much by what I can see. He must be though - probably a spy - foreigner maybe - even though he spoke to that young woman in Russian. Don't trust foreigners. Never know what they're up to. Still I mustn't be too choosy. They've got lots of dollars and sterling. That's what counts in the long run. It just shows though. You can't always tell about some people. Funny that. He doesn't seem to mind being shoved around by that pig of a policeman. I noticed that he smiled at that young woman. Nerve! He must be a foreigner or he'd know better not to smile. He doesn't know what these secret policemen are like. They've got something special up their sleeve for him I'll bet. If he shoves me again I'll maybe suggest a few things that might happen to him. I ought to feel sorry for him really. Poor sod! He's had it.

I know one thing. I'm not going to get a swig of vodka. I wouldn't get my seat back for one thing and I wouldn't put it past that ugly one to follow me out into the corridor. Men are all the same. Anything could happen. I know his sort. With a face like that it's the only way he could get a woman. I'll stay here and I'm going to stay awake. In fact I'm determined to stay awake for the rest of the journey - and I'm going to keep my mouth shut. Then there's that other thing. I don't want to think about it now. I hope it won't take too long.'

Chapter Four
Mikhail

It is not so easy to be a student in Russia, still less if you are a Russian. At least that's what Mikhail believed. But he shouldn't have been too surprised. He was a young man and like all young men was in a hurry to get to grips with the world. Life for him had so far been a series of problems that had to be tackled head-on. He couldn't be held responsible for the attitude of others. Society had to look out for itself and if necessary make way for a new order of thinking. He despised the system. He despised all systems that placed strictures on people, especially young people - like him. He had no politics to speak of, yet he liked to think of himself as a radical, a political free thinker. He wasn't really sure what such things justly entailed but the young are fond of wearing labels, the more outrageous and shocking the better. In the old days he would probably have been regarded as reactionary and have been shot for his trouble. He was harmless enough but like many of the young could only see things in stark silhouettes. There was no distance or perspective in his ideals. He just wanted to be different and shout his difference to the world. In that respect he was remarkably the same as any other young man anywhere else. He would not have believed it. He did not believe his teachers, or his parents, when they tried to reason with him. Reason was the last thing he wanted to hear. He had made up his mind that he was leaving the university. He felt he was being stifled by a system that fed and bred him like some battery hen. He wanted more freedom and the surety that his talents, once honed to a serviceable perfection, were not dissipated by being forced into some inconsequential and frustrating job like that of a tourist guide. He wanted more than that. He had also seen where such principles could land him, for he had seen several of his friends who had tried to baulk the system ending up as road sweepers - or worse. He did not want that to happen to him. That's why he got out before he was trapped, with a wife, a family and sundry other responsibilities, so that even to be a tourist guide would have seemed like redemption. He was afraid to become like one of those people who had given in or had prostituted their minds and talents. That's what he liked to believe and what he wanted the world to believe. The truth of the matter, and what a sordid truth it was, was that he had given it all up for the sake of money. That's why he was taking the night train to Moscow - for money, not principles. This was the first time he had ventured outside his native Leningrad. He was too excited to want to sleep, and besides the journey would give him time to reflect.

'Well. I'm glad that part is over. It makes me nervous just waiting, but now we're on the move I feel much better. I wonder what it will be like in Moscow. It must be better than Leningrad. There were no opportunities there. I wish some of my friends were with me though. We could really have had a good time.

I look at the others in the compartment. There are only three - all women. The only one anywhere near my age is cradling a baby in her arms. She looks too young to be married. But then there is the baby? Can't tell these days. She also looks scared. I don't blame her. I'm scared myself if the truth were known. She reminds me of Helen. That's best forgotten. Girls only complicate life. I daresay though I shall not be able to avoid them in Moscow.

I try to catch the eye of the young girl but she is too scared to look at anybody for long. Maybe when she is relaxed a little I might get a chance to talk to her. I'll wait and see. The other two are much older and couldn't be more different, to look at certainly. That one in the corner is quite a fearsome looking dragon. She doesn't approve of me. I can tell that straightaway. I don't think she approves of the others either. Not by her looks. She has a squashed sort of face like some ugly toy animal, with two buttons for eyes. She has the look of a peasant but I'm certain she isn't one. I can tell that by her clothes. They are not especially expensive but they are solid and very likely the best there was to be had in Leningrad - a waste of time on her though. She's got a shape like some square dumpling and not anywhere near as tasty as one. She's a nosey-parker I'm sure. She'd better keep her nose out of my business. I can't stand that type of person. As long as she doesn't talk to me I can put up with her I suppose.

Now the other woman, sitting on the same seat as me, is something else - very nice. The kind of woman that makes me sometimes wish - never mind that now. She's dressed very well and looks very sophisticated. I haven't seen many women like her in Leningrad. From Moscow I suppose. Perhaps they are better looking in the capital. I remember one female lecturer - but she was something else. The trouble with women is that they never seem to come in exactly the right circumstances. Now if that young girl opposite me looked like this other woman then I might be interested. If I were honest with myself I'd be just as scared of the attractive woman if she spoke to me as I would of the squashed face dragon in the corner. The attractive one smiled at me, a friendly smile, and it made me feel good. I just hope that she doesn't misunderstand my smile. She might be one of those sorts of women - expensive. She's well dressed and not in the usual Russian clothes. They're western styles. She must have plenty of money. Then why is she travelling on this train? I wonder what she actually does for living. Not that I really mind, even if she is one of those women. I suppose it is always possible that I might see her again in Moscow. I should have plenty of money by then. No!

Silly idea! Stick to my own age group. She must be at least thirty, much too old really. I'll bet she's got all those ultra conservative ideals. I bet she's even a member of the Party.

So much for my fellow passengers.

I lean back against the padded seat and just look into space. There is no point in looking out of the windows. I am too far from them anyway. I can see spots of lighting though, so we must still be in Leningrad or on the outskirts at least. The train is picking up speed and the lights get fewer. It's funny really - a city at night - like the sky in a way. All those dots of light actually represent some sort of life going on. It's strange to think that one speck of light out there in the blackness might be a family at a meal, or someone working, studying for exams. Or it might just be a street lamp. It probably is. There are not so many now and the train has certainly picked up more speed. I doubt if anyone else will come into the compartment now. Anyway it's only a four berth. There'd be no room for anyone else. I don't think that any of the females are going to use the beds. I hope not. I shall have to stay in the corridor, if the conductress will let me. Now there's another dragon. The world seems to be full of these dragon women. They're so bossy and rude, and if that isn't bad enough, they're so ignorant into the bargain. Best to ignore them all, even the young girl and her baby. She doesn't look too stable to me anyway. Can never tell with females, young or old. They're always expecting something from you, always measuring you, criticising or looking for weaknesses. Yes it's definitely best to ignore them. I'll just get some sleep. There's a long way to go yet.

As my head sinks comfortably into the padded seat and I try to snuggle into the corner I hear a noise in the corridor. It sounds like laughter. There must be others out there, probably some of the tourists. I cannot resist finding out so I ease back the sliding door of the compartment and without leaving my seat I lean my head outside into the corridor. Almost at once I wish that I hadn't. The conductress it seems has been indulging in some exchanges with several of the tourists further down the coach, something to do with the opening of a window.

Whatever it was she seems pleased at the interchange for she is now wearing a wide smile. With those teeth she looks even more like a dragon, and about to devour somebody. Then she spots me and her manner changes. She barks out something I do not quite catch but her tone is sufficient for me to quickly duck back into the compartment and slam the door shut. I won't do that again in a hurry. I know I am blushing and am sure that the others are looking at me. In fact I feel more disgruntled than embarrassed. The conductress obviously has one face for us, her fellow countrymen, but is quite prepared to show another to the American dollars and pounds sterling of the foreigners. As my feelings subside a little I can perhaps understand her reasons. After all I am only a poor student, not even that now. All I have are a few miserable roubles. I have already learnt that the hard currency of the West was becoming the great god of our society. I can't help smiling to myself though. Soon it will be my turn. A few miserable roubles indeed! If only she knew.

The train is moving quite fast and very smoothly. The dots of light have all disappeared. We must now be out of Leningrad and well on our way. I know it is a long journey and I am sure that I will doze off sometime. I am not particularly worried for I have entwined the strap of my rucksack around my leg so that no one can get it away from me without I wake up. Even though there are only three women in the compartment I don't trust any of them. You can never be certain about people. At the moment I don't feel sleepy although I half close my eyes. I peer through the lids as though I were in some way expecting the others to begin talking or moving, or doing something. They do nothing. They're a silent, dull lot. Is that the way women are? Not like men. If some of my friends were with me we could have a good old time. No, perhaps not. They were too worried about their exams, the future and what people would think. It just shows how the system can get to you.

I wonder how long we have been on the train. It is travelling at a fair speed now. As I think about the time, I notice that the attractive woman next to me has a similar thought for she suddenly pushes up the sleeve of her coat and glances at a small, but very smart, wristwatch. That must have cost a rouble or two I shouldn't wonder. Of course it is a mistake to look at it openly, especially with the square faced dragon in the corner looking on. If those button eyes were fingers I am sure that she would snatch it from her.

'That's a nice watch,' the dragon says, suddenly coming alive and leaning towards the attractive woman.

I could tell that what she really means is that it should be hers by right. She is that kind of person. She believes that anything, which takes her fancy, ought to belong to her.

'Where did you get it?' the dragon rasps in a voice like a damaged foghorn.

The attractive woman, I wish I knew her name, though obviously flustered keeps reasonably calm I think and says that it is a present.

The squashed face snorts in disbelief. 'I bet. For services rendered - in bed.' Then having hurled her insult she flops back into her seat.

If I understand the dragon correctly, she was hinting, no accusing the attractive wristwatch owner of being a prostitute. I cannot help but look at her, therefore, in a new light. For some odd reason I feel better about the idea of her being such a person. Perhaps in a way it makes her less remote and more like the rest of us - weak and grabbing. I feel that if I smile at her now it might convey some sort of friendliness and understanding. After all I am not so pure myself. It is well I don't for she gives me such a look. She is obviously annoyed, mostly with old squashed face, yet manages to convey something else in that look - a kind of warning. I vow right now to mind my own business totally and ignore all the goings on which might occur. I am right anyhow. Can't trust people - women especially. I wonder who sent that letter. Best not to think about it for the moment. After all, nothing may happen.

I wish it was daylight then at least I would be able to see something of the countryside we are passing through. I suppose it is best to sleep on the night train. There's nothing to see and even if the company was friendlier, people are usually too tired to want to talk. With my own friends it might have been different. I have never seen much of the countryside around Leningrad. I think my mother took me on a trip once, to see an old relative. I was too young to remember it properly. A pity. I should like to know what Russia really looks like. Still when I get to Moscow and meet up with the others, I'll get enough money to be able to go where I want - except out of Russia of course.

As I think and drool over all the possibilities Moscow has to offer I can feel myself drifting off to sleep. The gentle, metallic throb of the wheels is hypnotic and, with nothing much to concentrate on, it is too easy to succumb to their rhythm. Even the young girl opposite looks tired. She ought to get some sleep, especially with that baby to look after. Strange that it hasn't made a sound since we got into this compartment. I hope there's nothing wrong. In any case she looks worried enough for both of us. I shouldn't complain. I prefer a quiet ride. No sooner has that thought slipped into my mind when I hear a noise in the corridor. This time it isn't laughter. It sounds more like some kind of quarrel. The trouble with me is that I am one of Nature's inquisitive sorts and I am about to slide the door and have a look when I remember the conductress. I think better of it. I don't particularly want to cross her if I can help it. I know her type, a petty official. She would only mark me out as a troublemaker and would probably have the police onto me when we stopped. I certainly don't want anything to do with them, though perhaps more to the point, I don't want them to have anything to do with me. The first thing they would probably do, would be to search through my rucksack. As a student I will automatically be regarded as a doubtful type, almost like a criminal. It has happened to my friends so I know. I wouldn't stand a chance. No. I shall resist temptation. I don't care what's going on out there. The others don't seem to be too bothered either.

I sit back and fold my arms. I have no sooner done so when the door is violently slung back and the conductress stands framed in the doorway. It is too dim in the corridor to see if there is anyone else there but I do hear some scuffling and see some indistinct shadows, so I suppose there must be. The conductress doesn't say anything but just looks at each of us in turn. She is not very pleased. I can tell that from the look on her face. If she was a firing squad she could not look more menacing. I suspect though that it is not us that cause her to look so terrifying. I am right. She gives a sort of grunt and then as if by some feat of conjuring she produces a squirming, struggling figure of a man. She seems to be holding him around his collar but it is just a trick of the light. She is strong enough though. Out of the darkness, behind her, another person pushes his way into the compartment. It was a man, tall and big, and it is now clear that it is this bigger man who in reality has hold of the struggling one. He pushes him into the compartment and he stumbles against me before falling to his knees in front of the young girl with the baby. She gives a frightened squeak and almost jumps back in her seat.

The fallen man struggles to one knee and smiles at the young girl. "I...I beg your pardon," he stammers. "I'm clumsy."

The young girl points to his face. "You're bleeding," she says.

I hadn't noticed anything wrong with him but then I didn't really get a good look at his face.

If the young girl had looked scared before she is even more so now and she clasps her baby tighter as the small man struggles to his feet.

The big man then turns back to the conductress and says something to her. I can't hear what he says but I don't mistake his tone. The conductress isn't much pleased either. She still feels that she owns the train but this time it isn't a student she is dealing with but someone with much more authority than she has.

The whole episode has taken only a minute or so and I am more interested in events rather than the characters. This is due perhaps to the fact that I haven't seen either of these two intruders properly. However, when the big man steps fully into the compartment I can well understand the reason for the conductress's attitude. There is no mistaking the sinister form of a secret policeman. Dressed all in black, a kind of uniform with them, he presents a daunting figure to all of us. Suddenly I am scared. The last thing I want is to have to share my journey to Moscow with one of these dreaded persons. It now seems equally as obvious that the smaller man is his prisoner.

Instinctively, I ease myself as far back into my seat as possible and into the corner. I try not to look at either of them for fear of attracting their attention. The policeman pushes his prisoner down onto the seat and next to the dragon in the corner. He sits next to him. This move has the effect of provoking square face into life.

"No room in this compartment. Only for four." She emphasises her disquiet by some violent shuffling on her seat and would no doubt have pushed the smaller man off if he had been on his own. I must admit that I couldn't help agreeing with her on this occasion.

The policeman, of course, takes no notice and gives her a frozen stare, and then I notice for the first time what an extraordinary face he has. I always think it is old fashioned to say someone is ugly or beautiful. It is so trite. This policeman, however, possesses no attractive qualities, not even bearable qualities, that I can detect. He is like a man carved out of stone - badly carved. I try hard not to look at him but such features hold a strange fascination in a way a snake can mesmerise its prey. He takes his time in staring at each of us in turn as if he is trying to measure our criminal potential. I don't think that any of the women enjoy this. He tries to smile at the attractive one but it comes out all wrong. In any event she is not so put out by his thick-lipped leer. Her own look in return would have frozen most men. It changes his attitude a little and I think I detected, for a very fleeting moment, a touch of uncertainty in his features. It is as if he is unsure of himself. I know that feeling but then I am only a young student. I wonder why he was unsure. But it is only a momentary flicker. His face soon resumes its grim stoniness. Now he begins to look around at us again with a more leisurely, studied look. I try to be as inconspicuous as possible in such a small space, afforded by the compartment of a train, where I am one of only six passengers. I make a conscious effort not to do anything to attract that stony gaze to my corner. It is difficult to do nothing when you are concentrating like mad on doing it. Hands fiddle and feet shuffle while it is always a great temptation to turn the head. I wish now I had chosen a window seat. At least I would be able to look out into the blackness and pretend that I have nothing to hide. The trouble is though that I do have something to hide, and I have this terrible feeling that the policeman knows all about my secret. It is quite unreasoning but guilt is like that. The only thing I can do is to pretend that he isn't here - to ignore him. That is going to be difficult.

The compartment is quiet and the wheels of the train sound loud and coarse as the express rumbles on into the night. Nothing must go wrong but I have an uneasy feeling that it is going to be a very long night.'

Chapter Five
Natalia

Travelling is always difficult for a mother with a baby. Natalia knew this although she hadn't much experience about such things. She was almost a child herself. That is perhaps why she had decided to go to Moscow with her baby. She had not given the matter much thought. The only thought in her mind was to get away from Leningrad.

Natalia was no more than twenty years old, for which some girls is an age of maturity, even experience. But she was neither mature nor experienced. Had she been she would have stayed at home and continued her studies till she had learnt more about life and people. The baby? That was something else.

Natalia was not unattractive but physical and emotional upheavals had left their mark. She was a slimly built girl but her hollow cheeks and darkened eyes indicated that she had lost more weight than she could afford to lose. Her cadaverous appearance was perhaps enhanced by the wild, staring look with which she regarded everything and everyone around her. She looked afraid and nervous, almost on the verge of hysteria. Every new situation for her was fraught with fresh, unimaginable dangers. She had not thought much about what a long journey would mean for her and the baby. Nor had she given much thought to anything she had left behind. Her mind and heart were fixed only on getting away, and Moscow was the likely place. She had an aunt there. Aunts always understood. So that's where she would be going. Natalia had already written to her so she knew about the baby. She needed a place to rest and think. That had been her trouble. She had never given any thought to the future, but even so life had been all right until she met Boris. Yet her parents, teachers and friends had always regarded her as a sensible girl. But then people can change, especially if they meet other, more persuasive people. Boris was persuasive. He was older than Natalia, not by too much but he had knocked around a bit. Young, sensible Natalia had become completely enmeshed in his charm and had surrendered to his experience. Marriage had been discussed but somehow the thought of such a permanent arrangement frightened her, as did the idea of having sex with Boris, when he had suggested it. Of course she inevitably gave way to his charm and a baby was the result. There was no more talk of marriage though - and probably no more Boris either. Natalia was frightened and she was running away because she was frightened. So many things had happened to her in such a short time, terrible, frightening things. She couldn't cope with them all. The only thing she wanted to do at the moment was to run and run. She felt that she had to. The trouble with running away, however, was that people would come looking for her. When they find her, as they were sure to, they would make her go back. She didn't want that. She had to go on. She mustn't stop.

She had somehow managed to get a seat on the night train from Leningrad. She only wished that she could have had the compartment to herself. She could not bear the thought of people looking at her and asking questions - always asking questions. She wished...she wished...

'I wish I could relax. I'm sure the other passengers think that there is something wrong with me. Well, there's nothing wrong with me - nothing. I'd tell them if they asked. Why don't they ask? I feel so tired yet I must stay awake. I can't trust any of these people. They will only want to take my baby away.

I know they will. That woman in the corner looks like a busybody. She's got that sort of face. Think she knows better than anyone else. Well, she'd better keep her opinions to herself as far as I'm concerned, and as far as the baby's concerned. I bet she's never had a baby. Too self centred. I can tell from her podgy hands. It's funny but they're like a baby's hands only bigger. Always grasping at something and holding on to it. Yes – I'm sure she's like that. She's rude too. I saw the way she deliberately kicked that other woman. Pretending she couldn't get past. It was just a gesture of selfishness. She would have pushed me but for my baby. I'm sure of it. She's that type of person. The way she scrambled for that corner seat was like a spoiled, greedy child. If it weren't for the baby I would have told her so. The older generation! Huh!

I look across at the other woman, a very attractive woman. I bet she's not much better, in spite of her looks. She doesn't know that I am looking at her. I wouldn't look at any of them in the eye. They might think that I wanted their help or something - which I don't. This other woman is quite beautiful I think, with such lovely clothes. I wish I could be like her. She looks so sure of herself and does not seem to get flustered. I'm afraid of people all the time. I'm even more afraid for the baby. I won't let anyone touch it or even look at it. No. I mustn't let them do that. I wonder how long the train will take to get to Moscow. I hope it is not too long. I can't stand being in this compartment. It is choking me. I wish we were there now. That attractive woman is smiling at me. I nearly smile back at her. I mustn't become friendly. It will only start them asking questions. I don't like questions.

Then there's that young man sitting opposite. He's a student. I can tell. He doesn't look like Boris. This student looks much younger, about my age. I don't want to speak to him either. I don't trust students. I don't trust men - or boys. He will only want to see my baby and want to know its name. He's not really interested in the baby. He just wants to talk to me because I am a young girl. Well, I shan't let him. I won't even look at him. I know what he wants. I don't trust him. I don't trust any of them.

I want to lean back and close my eyes. I feel so tired. It must be quite late now, nearly midnight. If my baby wakes up I shall have to feed it. I shall go into the corridor. It looks so black outside. Perhaps it would be better if I did go out into the corridor anyway. I saw that student look outside and heard the conductress shouting at him. Serves him right. He asked to be shouted at. I don't like the conductress though. She's another busybody, always telling people what to do - just like my parents. Why can't they leave me alone? I'm tired. I just want to sleep. I look across at the window and I can see a kind of sparkling blackness flashing past. The lights look so strange. I suddenly want to be out there in that blackness, where nobody could know me or be able to find me. But there was that letter – something else to worry about.

That ugly woman is talking to the attractive one. I wish she wouldn't. Her voice is so harsh and loud. I'm sure that she will wake the baby. I don't want them to talk. I want them to be quiet. I shall go mad if they keep on talking. The attractive one has a nice wristwatch. Boris said that he would get me one of those but he never did. I would have liked one. It would have been something.

They are quiet now. The only noise is the clicking of the wheels as the train gets faster. I bet they think that I'm not married. I should have worn a ring. At least it would have kept them from prying. I know what they think. Those others don't wear rings, just wristwatches. The ugly one doesn't wear a ring or a wristwatch but she isn't the type anyway. I wish this journey were over. I can't stand being in this carriage. It's so crowded. I know that they are looking at me and wondering what I am doing on this train. I don't care what they think. They can't hurt me by thinking.

My thoughts are beginning to become jumbled and I suddenly feel very tired. The baby in my arms is growing heavy. I wish I could sleep, but I haven't been able to sleep for a long time now, not properly that is. I should like very much to doze off like the others. They all seem as if they are sleeping. I daresay though they are only pretending. They hope that I will go to sleep so that they can then talk about me and stare at my baby and me while I'm not looking.

Just as I make up my mind to doze off I hear a noise in the corridor. It's that conductress again. There are other voices and I can tell that they are quarrelling. Someone is coming after my baby and me. I am certain. I have nowhere to hide and the others won't help me. I can see that student looking at me again. He will open the door I know he will. He can't keep his big nose out of anything. I want to shout to him, to plead with him to keep the door closed. Don't let anyone in. They are coming after me. But the words stick in my throat.

I huddle my baby close to me. I know something terrible is going to happen. The others have also heard the noise and are awake and listening to what is going on in the corridor. The student now pretends that he isn't interested in what's going on out there.

Suddenly the door is opened and the conductress is there, staring at all of us. She looks at me and I know she is going to say something. I am terrified. But she doesn't speak. Instead it looks as though she is holding someone by the collar, another passenger, and a man. I don't want to look at anyone else. Why is she holding him? But then I see that it isn't the conductress who is holding this man. Another person comes from the darkness past her and pushes the man into our compartment. He stumbles over the student and falls on the floor right in front of me. I scream or something like that. I want to move away from him.

"I'm sorry. I beg your pardon miss," the man says as he struggles to his knees.

He is not a young man and he is very shabbily dressed but he tries to smile as he speaks to me.

"I am so clumsy."

He isn't clumsy. It is the fault of that person who pushed him and that stupid student who had his legs stuck out. I couldn't help giving another small scream. It isn't exactly a scream but I am too surprised to know what I am doing. I point at him.

'You're bleeding,' I say and I want to scream again, out loud. I want to get away from here but something stops me. I hold my baby tightly and try to scramble back against the seat away from all this.

The small, shabby man gets to his feet as the other one, a big man who looks very frightening, speaks to the conductress. She is angry. I can tell. I don't know what the big man is saying to her but he sounds angry as well. I can't help staring at him although I don't want to. He has finished speaking to the conductress and he steps into the compartment. He grabs hold of the smaller man and pushes him down onto the seat next to the ugly woman in the corner. She doesn't like it and I hear her complain. I don't like her voice. It is so harsh. The big man ignores her and then sits next to me. I move away from him into my corner. I don't want him to touch my baby. He looks horrible. I am frightened of him. He is like some cruel, evil tyrant. He is dressed in black and his face looks like one of those giants I used to read about in picture books when I was very young. He looks at everybody and then he looks at me. He has a big mouth with large, ugly teeth and I know that he has really come for my baby and me. The others won't help me because they will say that it serves me right. I could go into the corridor but he would only come after me. And then there is that conductress. She would shout at me and tell me to get back to my seat, just like she did with the student. I look across at the student but he doesn't notice. He is trying to look into the corridor. I think that he too is frightened of this big man. Maybe he has come to take him as well.

Everyone is so quiet now and the wheels of the train clatter loudly. It is very dark outside. I wish I were out there in the darkness. I cannot bear to be shut up in here all the way to Moscow. I don't know what to do. I am so frightened. I wish that I hadn't come on this train. I wouldn't have done except for that letter. I am trapped here. Everybody is after me, and my baby. I know now that it is a plot to capture me and take me back. They want to take my baby away from me but I shan't let them. I shall scream and fight. Oh Boris. What have you done to me? Why am I in such terrible danger? I didn't think it would be so awful. I must get away - I must. I will wait till they're not looking then I'll slip into the corridor. Yes. That's what I'll do. Or wait till the train stops. It must stop somewhere. I heard the conductress tell someone it stopped. I could get out and run off into the darkness. No one would know. They couldn't follow me then. I would be safe and my baby would be safe. I'll wait. That's what I'll do. I'll wait. I clutch at my baby and look around at the others. They don't see me looking at them. Good. I don't feel tired anymore, and when the time comes - when the time comes then I'll escape from them. I won't go yet though. I must wait for the proper time. I don't mind waiting. I've always waited. All of my life I've waited. Now I have my baby to think of. Then there is that other thing. I must be ready for that and make sure that I stay awake.'

Chapter Six
Vladimir Petrov

Vladimir Petrov was a secret policeman. He was not a very high up policeman, but then he didn't need to be. To be a secret policeman was enough in itself. His position in society allowed him many things that were denied to ordinary people, and he relished that position. It should be understood, however, that his loyalty to the Party was unswerving. Whatever the Party asked of him, he was proud to do. No job was too small or undignified. Yet for all that he was a man who enjoyed the pleasant things of life. Mostly he enjoyed the power his profession gave him over the ordinary people. He did not see it as a mere job as any other worker would. Like many in his 'profession', he often found himself in a position to sample some of the delights, which might otherwise have been difficult for a man like him to come by. All in all he felt that he had a good life.

Poor Vladimir Petrov he was, unfortunately for himself and those who had to look at him, an ugly man. It is said that ugliness is only in the eye of the beholder and a true heart and generous spirit will always shine out from even the plainest exterior of a person's face. It may be true. But it could never be proved in the case of Vladimir Petrov, for his ugliness was not merely skin deep but penetrated right through to his very soul. Then why 'poor' Vladimir? Because unfortunately for him he could not disguise his ugliness, nor did he try. Thus people could easily recognise him and shudder, not only at his face, but also at the man he was. Perhaps that is why he had never risen any higher in his chosen profession than that of an ordinary policeman. Yet strangely he enjoyed the fact that he could easily evoke a feeling of revulsion even in the most generous and tolerant of his fellow creatures. Those who employed him must have felt that he had a special gift, for his inherent twisted face and his unsavoury character made him eminently suitable for their purposes. He was often given all the most unpleasant tasks to perform, tasks with which the more fastidious members of the secret police did not care to involve themselves. It was not just a case of doing away with someone. They were all capable of that. In fact it is a prerequisite of the service that a member should not be squeamish, nor have any other loyalty. Nevertheless, there were situations that had their own particular brand of unpleasantness. Such situations might involve the interviewing of prisoners dying of an especially virulent and contagious disease; or maybe the torture of a child, the younger the better. The more the task outraged the sensibilities of those who feigned a certain delicacy of feeling, the more Vladimir Petrov relished it. He was immensely strong and powerful. He never caught any disease, nor did he suffer any remorse or the slightest twinge of conscience. He seemed to bear a charmed life among the festering dregs of humanity with whom he had to deal.

If he had a flaw, as a policeman, then it was that he was regarded as not being very bright. In fact it was surprising that he had lasted so long in the service for his mental capacity was only average and rarely matched situations in which he so often found himself. He certainly never came up to the expectations of those who employed him. He was more often taken for a fool, or at least he should have been, but unfortunately people never bothered to look beyond his face, which in its ugliness aroused more of fear for the appearance of the man than contempt for the man himself. In any event it is not always wise to wear any particular kind of face because there were always others who were prepared to read disapproval, disloyalty or downright treason in such ordinary displays of disgust. That was the trouble with a man like Petrov. It was not easy to disguise the abhorrence one instinctively felt at seeing him, especially for the first time. Of course it may have been different if he had not looked so much like a secret policeman, though it was not very probable.

Vladimir Petrov seemed to enjoy the general discomfiture and sense of fear that his presence generated. He liked it that way. In his own twisted fashion he had what he pleased to call a philosophy. This philosophy was centred on the fact that he truly believed that everyone, whatever station they commanded in society, was guilty of some crime or other. Whenever he had nothing better to do he would 'create' crimes for people. For the next few hours he had nothing better to do.

He looked around at the others in the compartment and began to think of suitable crimes, which would fit each of them. He enjoyed this kind of pastime and sometimes it brought surprising rewards. Many was the occasion when he had frightened an innocent person into admitting a crime by suddenly confronting them with it, proving to himself at least, that they were not so innocent. He prided himself upon his shrewdness, and the more lurid the crime the more he enjoyed it. As his heavy lidded eyes flickered over each passenger, he began to assemble in his mind a complete dossier of their transgressions, their sins against the state. He didn't bother with the small, shabby man at his side. He already knew all about him. But what about the others? His imagination began to work.

'That woman in the corner by the window looks suspicious enough. I wonder what she has in that bag which she protects with her legs so carefully. I'll bet it is the only thing she has had between those stumpy pins of hers. I can't see her with a man. What a sight! But I've seen worse. Those eyes and that face are a dead giveaway. She's hiding something, I'm sure of it, and very likely it's in that bag. Whisky? No. It would hardly be worth travelling with just a bottle or two, and to Moscow at that. She could have got just as good a price in Leningrad. What about watches? She could hide a lot of watches. But again why bother when she could do just as well by staying at home. She looks greedy though - for something. Roubles! That will be it. It's too hot for her in Leningrad so she's going to Moscow. I shouldn't be surprised if she's got a little gang already working for her in the capital. I know her type. She wouldn't do the dirty work herself. I bet she makes this trip at least once a month. I'm only surprised that she bothers. If she only knew that Leningrad is just as profitable these days. But greedy people are always stupid. Or maybe there's something else –

Now that one on the other seat - I don't have to think too hard about her. She's a prostitute if ever I saw one, though there is something odd about her. That look she gave me. For one nasty moment it reminded me of Major Ivanof. He looks like that when he's angry. She's a brassy tart all right, looks or no looks. She didn't come by those clothes honestly. They're much too good to have been bought in Russian shops. They're hard currency clothes, and that wristwatch. She must have come a long way from a few oranges. I shouldn't be surprised if she's the mistress of someone high up in the Party. That's it all right. It must be someone pretty important. That would explain the look she gave me. She thinks that she's safe from the likes of me. That's where she's wrong. I'd love to have her in the question room. I'd make her talk, and I'd make her do a few other things too. Yes, I would like that.

What about him in the other corner? There's a troublemaker for you. A student! They're all troublemakers. Always shooting off their mouths, those students. Let's see what he's guilty of. Bound to be something, else why is he travelling on this train? Besides if he is a proper student, why isn't he at university? It hasn't closed for any holiday. He's skipped it I bet. But why I wonder? That rucksack of his looks suspicious. He's got something in there. I know he has. What could it be though? Drugs? It has to be drugs. All students take drugs. I never met one that didn't. Yes, and I've broken a few students in my time. There's nothing they wouldn't do to hide their little pleasures. Beats me why they need them. They're supposed to be the brainy ones, the clever ones. Maybe that's what makes them clever. They can't be all that smart though. I always get them. On the other hand it could be something else. Books maybe. No. Pamphlets - underground writings. I've heard all about those things. These clever ones are always trying to run down the Party but they can't do it openly so we can get at them. They print things behind our back. I can't stand that kind of filth. I'll have him before we reach Moscow, along with those two women.

Who else is there? Ah - that young girl with her baby. Baby? Not very likely. I've seen too many 'babies'. They're just a convenient way of smuggling drugs, or food, or anything. Might even be a gun under all that wrapping. A terrorist. They have them in other countries. I've heard about them. These girl terrorists are the worst. She looks mad enough to be one of them, with those staring eyes. Well miss; we don't have terrorists in Russia, not while I'm about. Though if she is a terrorist, she's a bit skinny. Looks too young. Maybe she's in with that student there. They pretend not to know each other but that doesn't fool me. On second thoughts though she doesn't look the type. She looks too afraid, even of her own shadow I should think. That's it. She's committed some crime and she's running away. She's got a baby and there's nothing a mother wouldn't do for her baby. Where is her husband? Strange he isn't with her. She looks the kind who ought to have someone with her. Maybe she's crazy. It seems more likely that she's escaped from a hospital, from one of those crazy wards. Still, there could be a gun in that blanket. I shall keep an eye on her. I shall keep an eye on all of them. They all look suspicious and I bet I'm right about every one of them. We shall see. I shall probably end up with another four prisoners - unless any of them want to give me an argument.

At least another six hours before we get to Moscow. We must be somewhere in the countryside now. It is dark out there. I could easily get rid of them all. That nosey conductress will keep her mouth shut or I'll have to do something about it. Right then! Who shall I start with?'

Chapter Seven
Petrushka

He looked at no one but saw everyone. The insignificant, rather shabby little man seemed to be the only one in the compartment who did not in the least mind his surroundings. He wore a perpetual grin. Whether it truly revealed his inner self or not was hard to tell. Very likely it was due more to the odd upward twist of his mouth, that together with an unusually distinct ruddy complexion. Nothing could shake the twinkle from his eyes or that all-knowing smile which constantly fluttered about his lips, occasionally breaking into a large expansive smirk of joy and delight. Yet he had little with which to be delighted. As the much-abused prisoner of the big policeman he was the one who should have felt the reality of terror. The others in the compartment only imagined their terrors because of what they already carried with them. They each had their own little secret. But this small man had the greatest secret of them all.

If everything was to be believed about the secret police, the small man, whose names was Petrushka, was in for a rough time. Already he was a prisoner of perhaps the most brutal and implacable of all policemen - Vladimir Petrov. Though he must have been aware of his perilous situation, he showed no sign that he minded.

Petrushka was not his real name. His real name didn't

matter. In the sleazy and shadowy world in which he lived he was just known as Petrushka the clown. Oddly enough he was nothing like the lovesick clown of the Stravinsky ballet. He was much too jovial. It was his face and mannerisms, which had obtained for him the nickname, together with a reputation for playing jokes. The jokes he played were mostly at the expense of authority. Yet it would be difficult to say exactly how he had sinned against the establishment. He was neither a thief, nor spy, nor murderer; nor was he wanted for money changing or any sedition he may have preached against the state. For all that he was probably among the most wanted men, by the police that is, in the whole of Russia. Even among those who thought they knew him; he was regarded as a man of mystery. He never seemed to be involved in anything specific but whenever a writer or dancer defected to the West, it was always reported that a small, shabby man had been seen hovering somewhere in the background. Whenever a political prisoner disappeared or evaded the clutches of the police, Petrushka was said to have been involved. If all the reports from the underworld were to be believed, then this small, shabby, insignificant man known as Petrushka the clown, was a kind of Robin Hood and Scarlet Pimpernel rolled into one. Of course it is possible, and very likely, that he was nothing of the sort. From the looks of him, he could have been anything from a common pickpocket to a vagrant. But then there are no vagrants in Russia, and very few pockets are worth the picking. It was sufficient for the secret police to know that he looked like the kind of person who could and would commit crimes against the state. It may well have been that it was solely their interest in him that had in effect promoted him to a figure of mystery and the stuff of which legends are made. Now secure in the custody of that most hated policeman, Vladimir Petrov, no one would ever know. He was on his way to face - interrogation - torture - oblivion!

The man, known as Petrushka, didn't seem to mind that he was being taken to a place from which he would never return. His ruddy complexion shone with a knowing innocence. As he sat with hands on knees, he looked at the other passengers and beamed. It was a smile of reassurance for them rather than for himself. But nobody took any notice. They were all afraid to look at him. After all he was a criminal and any sort of sympathy shown on his behalf could only result in grave trouble for whoever expressed such sympathy. The little man didn't mind. He understood the way of things. Yet he wanted to assure them that all was not as it seemed. There was a long way to go before the night train from Leningrad reached Moscow and much could happen before then.

The train sped on, snaking through the night like a monstrous, metallic serpent. There was no belching of fiery smoke or hissing of steam to betray its presence. The only sound it made was the clitter-clatter of its wheels over the rails, and so fast was it now travelling, that even this noise had become one long subdued murmur of a monster in a hurry. Outside it was black. There was no moon to illuminate the vast snow strewn tracts, or the tall forests of pine and birch. Here in these forests, where the snow could not reach, it was darkest of all. Perhaps this monster was also afraid, and was rushing with all possible speed towards the lights of the next town, or towards the dawn. Both were equally as far.

Inside the last carriage most of the occupants were asleep, or trying to sleep. It was almost one o'clock. The foreign tourists had already experienced several busy days in Leningrad and were expecting more in Moscow. Despite the novelty of such a journey therefore, none of them wished to waste valuable sleep time. It was too dark to see anything, and one walk along the corridor had revealed all there was to know about their carriage. In the last compartment of the last carriage, however, no one slept. Neither was anyone speaking. They all sat silent with their own thoughts. No matter how tired they might feel, they could not risk the pleasure of a few moments of sleep. It might have been possible earlier, before the extra passengers had suddenly appeared, but not now. It was that policeman and his prisoner.

Each of the original passengers wanted to know more but each knew that they must not show the slightest interest in anyway whatsoever. They could only guess. Besides, they were grateful that it was the small, shabby man who was the prisoner, for each of them knew that it could easily have been them. That is not strictly true, for although they all possessed secrets only one of them had a secret, which involved identity. Whether such a secret, or indeed any of the other secrets, would come to light during the journey, only time and events would show. The small, shabby man known as Petrushka the clown knew all this. He knew all their secrets and what's more, he knew that before the journey was over, all their secrets would be spilled out like confetti. When those secrets were no longer secrets, then he would himself be free. He smiled to himself at the certainty of the knowledge. If he really did know anything at all, he knew people and he understood human nature. He was even sure of the big, stone-faced policeman. He was more certain of him than anyone. So again he smiled to himself and relaxed. All he had to do was to wait and it wouldn't be too long now. He looked around once more at his fellow passengers, hoping to catch them off guard with a smile of encouragement. There was no response. He even turned to the big policeman. He didn't smile at him but he knew from the twitching muscles of the face and the licking of those thick lips, that he wouldn't have long to wait. Petrushka was quite content to lay back and close his eyes. He would open them again when it was time.

Chapter Eight
First Accusation

It is now one o'clock. The train speeds onwards, its single eye cutting a path through the thick darkness. Like some great, whispering dragon it silently and swiftly devours the miles but, not quickly enough for the six passengers in the last compartment. None of them can wait for the journey to end, for each had a special reason for wanting to reach Moscow as soon as possible. So they sat in watchful silence. They did not look at each other but were aware that they were always under scrutiny. Four of the passengers were now experiencing an atmosphere becoming heavy and oppressive with menace and danger. It had become so real that it was almost suffocating in its effect. This journey would soon develop into a ride of terror. They knew this instinctively but, with the notable exception of the policeman, they were resolved to do nothing to make the situation worse. Not even the truculent Olga, or the nervous girl with the baby, was disposed to voice their growing unease.

It is the policeman, Vladimir Petrov, who breaks the silence. He had now completed his summing up of the other passengers and had in his own mind assigned a crime to each of them. It was time to confront them each in turn and see what transpired. At the very least it would give him some hours of amusement. He could spin out the remainder of the journey in this way.

He enjoyed watching people squirm, and he didn't see why these people, here in this compartment, should not be part of the fun. His fun. He grinned at the thought.

The small man at his side suddenly awoke from his brief slumber. He too could sense that something was about to begin. He wanted to warn the others in some way but couldn't think how to do it. He could only wait. His fate was sealed anyway. At least it looked that way, but he might have a chance to do something. He knew this policeman and had been on his track for some time. But now he was Petrov's prisoner. He grinned at the irony of it all.

Vladimir Petrov leaned slightly forward and looked around at the others. "You are a quiet lot. Why don't you speak? Say something? Ah, I forgot. It is late and you are tired I suppose. Yes. I understand." He spoke in short bursts, with a pause between each statement as if to allow for a reply. If that was the case, he was to be disappointed because nobody took any notice. He sat back against the seat and allowed his heavy features to break into a smile.

"Ah! You were speaking to one another before I came into this compartment. But now you have stopped." He paused. "Why? I want to know." He paused again. "Yes - I want to know," he repeated, but this time with a harder edge to his voice.

Olga, the square faced woman in the corner, slowly turned away from the window, through which she had been steadfastly gazing for the last half hour, and looked at him. "It is late. We are tired and we wish to get what sleep we can. I'll thank you to mind your own business." With that she turned back to her window gazing.

The policeman must have thought her remarks were amusing because he suddenly laughed aloud. "And I thought it was because of me and my friend here. I have that effect on people you see. They don't speak when they see me. Not until I make them speak that is. Just because I am a policeman."

"You're a policeman are you?" Olga said, affecting a

deliberate indifference in her tone. "Then you are probably right. That's the reason no-one speaks." She had not looked away from the window while she was talking.

"Yes," said Vladimir Petrov slowly, "a secret policeman."

It seemed that he expected such news to have an immediate and paralysing effect on the rest of them but again there was no response.

The small, shabby looking man known as Petrushka chuckled. "You really are a fool Petrov. Everyone can see that you're a secret policeman. It sticks out as much as that ugly face of yours."

Vladimir Petrov scowled and, with a muted snarl, viciously dug his elbow into the small man.

Petrushka just winced and continued to smile.

"Well?" Vladimir Petrov said loudly and threateningly. "I am a secret policeman, and this man is my prisoner." He underlined the fact by another vicious dig into the unsuspecting ribs of the small, shabby man. "Get over there, where I can see you better," he growled and shoved the small man across to the opposite seat.

The small, shabby man seemed happy to comply and despite the two vicious blows he had just received, still managed a small smile.

The policeman's words and actions had only mildly interested the others who slowly turned to regard him. They showed no special fear in their eyes and this was beginning to annoy Vladimir Petrov. The young girl didn't even look at him properly but just kept cooing to her baby as if it might wake at any moment.

Rather than show any sign that he was not pleased, the policeman relaxed into a smile once more. He said nothing for a moment or two. He was carefully weighing up his words for he wanted them to have the right and proper effect. When he spoke, his words were carefully innocent, and yet he managed to convey a silken, indefinable menace as he spoke them.

"I have a game I play when travelling on long journeys like this. It helps to pass the time." He chuckled to himself. "I don't suppose you can guess what it is?" He waited for a reply or some sort of reaction, but none came. He chuckled again and leaned back against the padded seat behind him. "Do you know what I do?" He licked his lips and allowed his eyes to flicker swiftly around the compartment. He was trying his best to savour this moment but somehow his words and soft approach were not working. "I try to guess what sort of tricks my travellers get up to. I like to work out what sort of crime you might commit or in fact have committed. That is if you were the kind of persons who would commit crimes." He paused and looked at each one in turn, with a half sneering smile lingering on his thick lips, calculated to encourage the right balance of uncertainty and fear. "Everyone has secrets, comrades, and I'm sure that you all have your fair share. I think I know what they are."

His face suddenly set and his jaw clamped tight as he allowed his eyes to flicker once again around the small assembly. Like a black Sphynx, all-powerful and all knowing he waited for those first signs that his words were having an effect.

The other passengers looked away from him and at each other. All sorts of ideas and thoughts were going through their minds. Did this policeman really know anything or was he guessing? But the secret police always knew so much. Should they confess, and if so to what and how much? Should they try and direct his gaze to someone else, and point out their suspicions about the others? But they realised that only those who did have something to hide would have entertained such thoughts. Nevertheless, these were only fleeting thoughts because each one of them knew that a secret policeman didn't need any help from informers. This man looked quite capable of making up his own accusations and, like many of his kind, would act as judge and executioner if it suited his purpose.

Petrov the policeman noted with satisfaction what he thought were the first signs of uncertainty, maybe even fear, creeping into their eyes. It amused him and he knew that he was going to enjoy this game. Who should he start with? It didn't really matter for he had plenty of time to deal with them all - perhaps that one in the corner, the ugly woman. She had already been a little too free with her comments. She needed a lesson. He turned towards her and leered. She quickly turned away to concentrate on the blackness of the window.

"Why do you look out of the window? It is much too dark to see anything surely?" Petrov asked in a sly, insinuating way.

Olga just grunted.

"Or perhaps you look out there because you do not wish to look at me. Do you think I am ugly?"

A slight twitch of her shoulders was the only answer Olga was prepared to make.

"That is it. You cannot bear to look at me." Petrov laughed quietly but there was no humour in his laugh. "I used to think that was the reason people did not look at me. Once I used to think that, but not now. You see I have since discovered that people turn their heads away from me because they were afraid to face me, to look me in the eye, so to speak. And do you know why?" He waited for Olga to say something but her face remained fixed to the window and she totally ignored his words.

"Perhaps it is because they had something to hide," Petrov continued smoothly, unruffled by Olga's lack of response. "I think that, perhaps, you have something to hide."

The square figure of Olga slowly turned to face him. She gazed at him steadily for a while, her eyes screwed up in an effort to outstare him.

Petrov was unmoved. He did not even blink.

"What makes you think that I have something to hide?" she said at length, her voice conveying a mixture of truculence and suspicion.

"Everyone has something to hide," Petrov said calmly and almost pleasantly.

"Well I don't!" Olga snapped and turned back to the window.

The policeman was not to be put off so easily. He knew that they all started out this way, with violent denials and obdurate refusal to admit to anything, but they gave way in the end. This ugly crow would also give way. After all he had only just started the game. There was still a long way to go and he didn't want to end it too soon.

"You're not going to leave it at that are you Comrade Petrov?" The small, shabby man suddenly spoke up. "You are going to persist in your interrogation? You always do." His eyes were bright and twinkling with some kind of secret joy. The others couldn't be sure whether he was mocking the policeman or maybe urging him on. It was difficult to tell with this Petrushka, whose bruised face really did make him look like a circus clown. He looked at the other passengers, who by now were showing a greater interest, though not much liking, in the policeman's questions.

"He's good, this Petrov, one of the best. He can get anything out of anybody." The shabby man leaned forward and looked at the others then lowered his voice to a confidential whisper. "He's reckoned as about the best there is." He sat up straight again and beamed a big smile. "You should feel honoured that you are about to witness the great Petrov at work - and at close quarters."

The others seemed as unmoved by the small man's words as they were by those of the policeman.

"They don't seem very impressed by your recommendation," Petrov said slowly. "I think you should have told them more. Like - my methods for example."

Olga turned from the window. "I'm not interested in you or your methods. I have nothing to hide. You may be a policeman, but you have no jurisdiction here. I am a law abiding citizen and a Party member, and I know my rights."

"You are speaking for everyone?" Petrov enquired.

Olga sniffed and clamped her mouth tight. "I don't know about anyone else," she said after a while. "I can only answer for myself."

"Bravo," said Petrov in mock approval. "That's all I ask of you, to speak for yourself. The others will then speak for themselves - later." He looked at her steadily but she did not seem to want to say more. He then glanced at the bag between her feet. "Is that all the luggage you carry with you? Not much is it?"

For the first time since she entered the compartment Olga, with the dour, squashed features, betrayed a sign of alarm and uncertainty.

Petrov pretended not to notice though he could barely conceal the delight he felt at seeing the first crack appear in this woman with the ugly face. In fact it had been his intention all along to focus attention on the bag. It was too obvious for it not to be true. People were getting clever. By looking so conspicuously like a criminal they thought that they might deceive the police and get away with things. Not with Petrov they didn't.

"The bag, comrade." He pointed to the bag. "What does it contain then? Something to eat on the journey? Something to drink? Vodka maybe? Why not share it with your fellow passengers?" He pretended to reach into the bag but quickly Olga snatched it up from between her legs and hugged it close to her chest, like it was a child.

"You mind your own business and I'll mind mine." Her pig-like eyes flashed angrily and her square jaw set itself in an attitude of Churchillian defiance.

Petrov was not deterred and he relentlessly continued with his probing, ignoring the others who now began to watch but without saying anything.

The others knew it would be their turn soon enough and were only interested in seeing how much resistance Olga could put up against the policeman's persistent questioning.

"There must be something valuable in that bag. I should like you to show me. You could prove me wrong."

Olga said nothing but her uncertainty was now evident to all.

"Shall I tell you what you have in there?" Petrov spoke softly but also in the sureness of his diagnosis. Soon he thought to himself. Soon.

Olga just shook her head. Her defiance had weakened and was now no more than instinctive stubbornness.

The big policeman had done nothing physical to her but she was beginning to feel the pressure of his questioning. Her resentment was still apparent, however, and she had sufficient of her wits to try and parry his constant probing. "Why don't you ask the others what they are carrying in their baggage? They've got plenty to hide I bet." She snorted and clasped her bag even tighter.

"Oh I will," Petrov said calmly. "I certainly will. Never fear," he added with a hint of menace. "Meanwhile I am much more interested in what you have in your bag."

The squashed like features of Olga didn't change. Her eyes just stared blankly ahead. She wasn't going to help this policeman. She knew moreover that it was no game he was playing. It was always the same with his lot. They just picked on people for their own amusement. It didn't matter to them what trouble or misery they caused, but she wasn't going to give in to him. He could do nothing to her - not here anyway; and if he was going to play the same tricks on the rest of them he would have his hands full by the time they reached Moscow. That miserable apology for a husband would have given in long ago. He was weak. She would like to see him undergoing such an ordeal. She compressed her lips firmly and hugged the bag tightly to show her resolution.

There was a strange new silence in the compartment, heavy with anticipation. The others had by this time become fascinated by the drama unfolding before them. For a while they could be spectators but soon they knew that each of them would be as deeply involved as the luckless Olga. They knew, even if she didn't, that Petrov the policeman had not yet finished with her. Their fascination was primitive and totally absorbing. No one felt that they wanted to be the first to break the spell, even supposing any of them could. It was as if Olga were acting as a champion for them all. If she succeeded then they would all succeed. But they were also sure that Petrov was only just beginning. Their anxieties were fast becoming fears. For a while, though, they could still retain some objectivity - at least till it was their turn. Their fears were based on their own secrets, and they all had secrets.

Meanwhile the train rushed onwards, eating up the miles. It was still black outside and to those in the last compartment it was like being suspended in time in some great, dark limbo. They could not escape. They could not even go into the corridor and to the next carriage. They felt that they had been drawn here by some unknown force and were now in the presence of some all-powerful inquisitor. The movement of the train and the darkness had combined to create a mesmeric effect upon them. It had robbed them of any will to co-operate with and to support each other. They were just individuals and would have to work out, each for themselves, their own salvation as best they could.

Petrov sat back on the seat. A slight, supercilious smile creased his face and gave him the appearance of some dark, vengeful angel - except that he was no angel. He would dispense justice alright. But the only concession he made to justice was that it would be meted out in exact quantities to all. The actual form of his justice was usually torture or death - or both. He looked across at Petrushka. "Tell her. Tell them all what I can do. What I shall do. You know, don't you, Petrushka. Tell them that it is useless to resist the inevitable."

The small, shabby man was no longer smiling. He had known from the beginning that the game being played by Petrov was going to continue until he had broken one or all of them, just as he had been broken. He was broken alright in spite of his smile and his air of disinterest. There was no fascination in the game for him. He had seen it all before. He spoke slowly and soberly.

"It always starts with the questions. Nothing too serious or threatening - not at first. But the questioning goes on and on and on. You think you will go mad. You confess to anything that will stop the questions. You admit to things that you think he wants to know, but the truth of it is that he is not interested in your answers only in how you make them." He spoke flatly and unemotionally, not looking at any of them. He was in a trance almost as he remembered his own ordeal. "He is not interested in your petty crimes, your sins against the state. He is only interested in breaking you and making you grovel. He wants you to become less than him because only then will he have a reason for his existence. Without that he is nothing."

"If that is the case, why didn't you deny him?" Irina, the attractive woman suddenly spoke.

Petrushka turned slowly to look at her and gave a weary smile. "Because he is strong and I am weak."

"But there are four of us - five counting you. He cannot harm us all." The student Mikhail, encouraged by the attractive Irina, was almost on his feet until he looked across at Petrov, who was slowly shaking his head and pointing a heavy service revolver at him.

"You see what I mean." The small man chuckled. "He is stronger than us - one way or another."

"Shut up you." Petrov snarled at the small man, then more pleasantly addressed the others. "I don't really need this." He waved the gun in his hand as if it was and obsolete toy and it produced the effect he knew it would. "I just thought you would like to be sure that I carried such a weapon. I might also have another one somewhere," he added absently and patted his pockets as he pretended to look. "It is not important." He put the revolver into his pocket and caressed the bulge. He smiled at them but his smile was not one of reassurance.

Although he had not directly pointed the revolver at her, Olga felt the threat behind the exhibition of it. She began, for the first time, to show some real alarm in those pig-like eyes of hers. They flitted about like a ferret's as her mind tried to put together some plausible framework of a story. Despite the sinister Petrov, she was determined not to reveal or surrender more than she had to. "If you must know," she muttered at length, "it's vodka." She fumbled noisily in her bag and produced a bottle of the colourless liquid. She handed it to Petrov. "Here. Take a swig of it if you don't believe me."

Petrov took the bottle, a half litre, and looked at it. He then looked steadily at Olga. "Only half full. Drunkenness is also a crime but we shall leave that for the moment." He unscrewed the top, took a sniff and then replaced the cap on the bottle. "It is vodka. Do you have more?"

Olga shook her head and mumbled something, which was not audible.

Petrov leaned towards her and waved the bottle in her face. "Is this all you have? Is this what you protect so fiercely? I doubt it, comrade." There was no smile on his face now and his voice had lost its former pretence of friendliness. "What else are you hiding in that precious bag of yours?"

"Nothing," Olga muttered, but with noticeably less defiance than before.

She turned to the others but her squashed up face would not allow itself to express any anxiety, or even a plea to her fellow passengers for intercession.

"Well. Don't just look. Tell him. He can't just come onto this train and start asking these questions and poking his nose into other people's business. Tell him! He doesn't have the right." The words came out all wrong. She hadn't intended to say exactly that, neither had she intended that she should say them in such a peremptory manner, not calculated to win anybody to her side. That was the trouble with poor Olga. She couldn't be nice even when she wanted to be. Rudeness and self-interest were so ingrained in her personality that she could not change now, though her life may well depend upon it.

The others, apart from not being won over by her outburst, were as much concerned with their own fate when their turn should come, and could spare little sympathy for people such as Olga. It was like that sometimes with people who live in a society where secret policemen have the power and authority of a seigneur or samurai warrior. Olga must struggle as best she may. No one would help her. No one would dare to help her.

Petrushka looked at Olga and then at the others. "He may not have the right but he has the power. Rights are not for people. They are just words spoken by the pious individuals who speak them from a safe distance. They are not here in this carriage." The small, shabby man spoke quietly and with no hint of accusation in his voice. His calmness was as chilling as the policeman's menace.

An atmosphere of doom and inevitability settled on the compartment and its occupants. The game must now be played out to its conclusion and Petrushka's words had the effect of making them all aware that they had become unwitting and unwilling players in this game. Petrushka knew this from the beginning but was not sure that the others yet realised it.

If Petrov realised it, he was not bothered one way or the other. His natural instincts and his talents would not be denied. As he was neither troubled by conscience or feeling, he saw no reason why he should not pursue his profession in whatever way or in whatever place he chose. He had already made up his mind that he would break each one of them before he reached Moscow, in the same way that another person would endeavour to complete a crossword puzzle in the same time.

"I do have the power. For once you are right, Comrade Prisoner," he rasped. "Now shut up." He turned to Olga once more. "What else, comrade? What else do you have in that dirty, scruffy bag that you are so unwilling to share with the rest of us?"

Olga was clearly ill at ease and could do no more than shake her head and mouth silent words to herself. Her grip never relaxed and she would not look at the policeman.

Petrov was a big man, bigger than average and, like many big men in such a profession, oozed power and strength. He didn't need to use any kind of physical force - not for most of the time. He didn't need to use it now. He only had to shift his great bulk closer to the hapless Olga for her to exhibit real signs of fear. He pointed to the bag.

"Open it up! Let's see what you are hiding with such an animal obstinacy," he said sharply and officiously.

Olga was by this time visibly upset though her features resembled more the aspect of a hound being led away by the local dogcatcher. "Nothing," she murmured quietly. "Nothing - nothing – nothing!" she repeated in a rising crescendo of fear, panic and sudden capitulation to the probing of this sinister man. As her voice was reaching a raucous shout she was at the same time shaking her bag in time with her denial. Unfortunately this resulted in making her lose control of it and suddenly the bag tumbled to the floor at the feet of the policeman with some of its contents spilled out. This had the effect of stopping her protests. She hastily bent forward to retrieve her belongings. She was too late.

Petrov had finally shaken that determination and now it was his turn to profit from it. Before Olga could gather her possessions and get hold of the bag the policeman, under the guise of assisting her, contrived during a brief struggle to spill the remainder of the contents onto the floor.

Olga gave a strangled cry. With a feverish scramble she was on her hands and knees desperately trying to sweep the various articles back into the bag. But her anxiety prevented her from doing the job properly, plus the fact that Petrov, still under the pretence of helping, was examining each article.

"More vodka." He held up another bottle. It was smaller than the previous one and it contained a darker liquid.

"No!" Olga almost screamed and made a grab for it. "It's – it's mine. It's my medicine. I have a heart condition." Her blotchy, purple features seemed to confirm the statement.

Petrov was not impressed with her explanation and proceeded to withdraw the cork and sniff at the contents. He made no comment and put the bottle to one side. As Olga went to grab it again he gave her a hard push, which sent her banging into the side of the carriage where she sprawled into an untidy heap.

"No - no," she began to whimper.

Ignoring her plea Petrov then casually began to examine the various items on the floor.

If a person's life was to be measured by the contents of their luggage, which they carried on a long journey, then Olga didn't have much of a life. The pathetic contents amounted to no more than a few trinkets; a woollen jumper; a few items of cheap, old-fashioned underwear and a small package. It was not really a package but more like a large envelope into which letters and other scraps had been stuffed. These were now tumbled to the floor by Petrov. He quickly sorted through them and then with a sudden grunted exclamation he picked out something from amid the mess of paper.

Olga did nothing to stop him though she did choke back an impulse to make some outburst as she saw what the policeman now held in his hand. She knew that it was all over. Everything was finished and she realised with a dreadful suddenness that her hopes and dreams were now gone. She began to sob quietly, with her hand over her mouth, and made no effort to get up from the floor. Like a whipped cur she remained slouched in her untidy, sprawling position and only allowed herself a few fearful glimpses at the towering black figure of the policeman.

Petrov stood up triumphantly clutching a tight wad of paper in his hand. He held it up like a trophy for the others to see.

"This is what I was looking for. Roubles. Over five hundred of them I should think." He flicked through the bundle to emphasise the quantity and thus the enormity of the crime.

"So what?" the young student muttered quietly, to himself rather than to the threatening figure of the policeman.

Petrov did not take offence. Instead he smiled, his large toothy smile, with lips curling back in a most unnatural manner. "Maybe a thousand roubles," he said with some relish. "And what are the likes of you doing with so much money? You didn't come by this honestly." He looked down at the cowering Olga. "Well?"

"Mine - savings – it's mine."

The words came out in between stifled sobs of self-pity but Petrov wasn't really interested in any explanation from her, not when he had one of his own.

"Too hot for you in Leningrad eh? You were on your way to Moscow to play your little game." He then addressed the others. "You see, this pathetic creature here robs the state, the people that is - you and me. She does it by selling roubles to the foreigners. The hard currencies like American dollars, or German marks or English pounds fetch a high price in the right places." He flicked through the bundle again and nodded appreciatively. "Not bad. She could have turned this little lot into maybe ten thousand roubles in a matter of a week or so."

The others looked and listened like students taking in a lecture, which was scheduled as a compulsory part of their course. They were not really interested in the economics of the situation or indeed the criminal aspect. From what the policeman said, and from the evidence in his hand, it seemed clear enough that the square faced Olga was a criminal of sorts. Her own capitulation and weak denial confirmed the fact. But none of this really mattered to them.

Of the others, Irina was tempted to say something to the policeman on behalf of Olga, but she didn't want to be drawn into the game, not till it was her turn.

Mikhail, the student felt much the same. In fact the unmasking of the dragon had only made him more fearful of his own predicament.

The young girl, Natalia didn't want to think of anything. She stared ahead and clutched her baby even tighter.

The only response came from the small, shabby man, Petrushka the clown. He clapped his hands, slowly and deliberately in mock applause and looked directly at Petrov with a big smile on his face. "Bravo, Comrade Policeman. We should be grateful that there are such men as you to protect us from the desperate criminal element in our society."

Petrov just scowled and without another word slipped the wad of notes into his pocket. He then sat down and contemplated the other passengers. He was no longer interested in the ugly one, the one with a square face and body to match. He had broken her and won the first round of his game. He leaned back and clasped his hands in contentment. They were large, indelicate hands, and might better belong to a woodcutter, or a smith - or a policeman. He clasped and unclasped his fingers as he pondered his next move. Who would be next?

The others had remained silent throughout the ordeal of the luckless Olga. If they had wanted to interfere they could only have done so at some great risk to themselves. They each had a secret to be revealed. Secrets they wished to keep to themselves. Yet they didn't really fancy being put through the same sort of interrogation as that of the square faced woman in the corner seat. At the moment she still lay on the floor with her paltry possessions scattered around her. She had stopped sniffing and turned an occasional frightened face to the others.

"You won't take it any further comrade?" the small, shabby man asked quietly. "You have done enough. You have the money."

Petrov grinned. "Yes. I have the money. But that isn't important. The criminal must still be punished."

"Why?" Petrushka asked.

"A crime has been committed. The guilty have to be punished. That is the way of it," Petrov said calmly.

The small man grunted. "You've got me. Why do you bother with them? They are nothing to you."

Petrov stared at the prisoner thoughtfully. "It is simple, comrade. I have you. Now I want them. Besides I am enjoying the game. It helps to pass the time." He turned to the others and leered. "You are all part of the game. I promise that I won't leave any of you out of it."

"I'm sure you won't." It was the attractive Irina who had spoken and immediately Petrov fastened his gaze on her.

Petrov was used to all sorts of women and he had no great feeling one way or another about them, even the more attractive ones. Nevertheless it pleased his vanity that this one was good looking. He had become fed up with the square, dog-like features of the other one.

All sorts of ideas ran around his mind and for a moment, just a brief moment, he wished he could have had her on his own, without the rest of them. Maybe later. The moment passed however. As far as he was concerned beauty was no more than another deception practised by criminals to hide their criminality. He had known many women who thought that they could fool him by flaunting their looks and their bodies in front of him. Fools. If they only knew what he really thought, they would save themselves the trouble. For all that he was a man and had had his share of female flesh, especially once he had broken them. And yet he had always felt that there was something missing. Nevertheless, he prided himself on knowing all their little tricks. No doubt he would continue to take his pleasures when and where he felt, and an attractive woman is always better than an ugly one.

As he gazed at Irina he was aware that there was something about her that troubled him. He had met many whores in his time and they mostly fell into a general category. Good clothes, heavily made up, money and a certain brashness, even coarseness, were the main features of such women. This one fitted the usual pattern and yet - "As you are so keen to be involved in my little game I think that you can be next." He shifted his large frame across the seat so that he now sat facing her. He leaned forward slightly and gave a leer. "What do you have to hide I wonder?" He licked his lips as he contemplated the shapely thighs of this woman and thought how he would take his pleasure of her - later. But first the game must proceed.

Chapter Nine
Second Accusation

Irina had plenty to hide but it was certain she would never reveal anything to the ugly Petrov. She knew his type only too well and perhaps realised better than the others what he really was capable of doing. By suddenly speaking during the uncomfortable lull after the interrogation of the square faced woman, she hoped that she would be able to draw most of his attention upon herself and away from either of the two younger passengers. Although she partly sympathised with the square faced woman, she could not feel any real sorrow for her. After all it was her own fault. If it hadn't been this policeman it would have been another one in Moscow, sooner or later. At least here on the train she had a chance to avoid prison. Even so, she had felt like interfering more than once but had held back because of her own secret. How long she could stall this man Petrov and play his game she wasn't sure, but at least it would eat up some time. Unconsciously she looked at her wristwatch. It was approaching half past two - nearly half way to Moscow.

"Nice watch," Petrov suddenly said.

"Yes, isn't it." Irina held out her arm so that he could get a closer look.

Petrov took her wrist and scrutinised the watch and then looked at her. He didn't relinquish his grip, which Irina found to be quite firm.

"I've always wanted a watch like that but a policeman's pay is not much."

"Take it, if you like it," said Irina, trying to sound casual but already the tightening grip of this man was making her feel nervous.

Suddenly he flung her arm away from him. "Are you trying to bribe me?" he snarled. "Better people than you have tried that. Not that it did them any good."

"No - of course not," stammered Irina. She blushed slightly but only because she realised that she had miscalculated about this man. She was aware that most policemen, especially the secret ones, were very susceptible to bribes. It didn't always work but she was confident that at least policemen were always tempted. Petrov was not tempted. He was different in that respect, or perhaps he just took whatever he wanted and when he wanted. He had already pocketed the bundle of roubles.

Petrov sat back on the seat and once more clasped his hands together in a self-satisfied manner.

Irina couldn't help thinking that as he sat there like that he reminded her of some overbearing inquisitor who could afford to let the accused sweat while he took his time about making his own considered judgement. It was power at its most naked, and Irina recognised that this man Petrov knew he had that sort of power and would exercise it at a whim.

"How can someone like you afford such a watch when I, a humble servant of the state, cannot? Eh?"

Petrov had begun his questioning.

"It was a present," she said simply.

"From an admirer." Petrov nodded as if pretending to understand.

"From a friend," Irina mumbled. She could already feel the build-up from the innocuous questions to something much more searching and accusatory. She would have to try to deflect this man and perhaps take some of the sting out of him, but first she must know what he intended to accuse her of, so that she could plan her defence. Although she was better equipped than the others to answer his questions she also knew that she possessed the greater secret and must therefore be extra careful.

"Do you have many such friends?"

She could now see what he was getting at. Well, if he wanted to think that she would not disillusion him, just yet. "I have several friends. There's nothing wrong in that is there?"

"No of course not." Again Petrov pretended to understand. He still clasped and unclasped his hands while making up his mind what his next question should be. "Do they all give you such expensive gifts - or do they pay you in other ways?" He looked at her coldly and there was no doubt in his eyes as to what he meant by this question.

Irina pretended not to understand, however. "I don't know what you mean. I sometimes get presents from my friends."

"You know very well what I mean. I may be a policeman but that does not mean that I am stupid. For services rendered." He spoke the last phrase as if quoting from some well-thumbed text, which of course he was.

Again Irina pretended not to understand his meaning. She wanted the interrogation to last as long as possible but it was going to be difficult for her to manage this as she sensed that the policeman was on the point of making an accusation.

"I'm sorry I don't understand you."

Petrov grinned but it didn't mean that he was amused, rather the opposite. "Oh yes you do, comrade. You understand very well." Suddenly and without warning he leaned forward and grabbed her wrist and held it tightly. The suddenness of the action made Irina cry out with the pain. He was still grinning but the fierce look in his eyes indicated that he was not playing and intended her to feel the pain.

In all his interrogation of the square faced Olga, Petrov had not once touched her, apart from one shove. He had destroyed her with questioning alone. With the attractive Irina it would be different. He would enjoy the use of force with her. With Petrov there was something about the attractive, the rich and the successful that made him want to crush them. He wanted to make them feel that their world could be made less comfortable - much less comfortable. Or maybe it was Petrov himself. A plain woman aroused nothing in him. She was just a case, a criminal statistic. Someone like Irina, however, was entirely different. It pleased him to see her squirm in pain. It gave him a much sharper sense of pleasure and power to see the cold, remote beauty crumple before his strength. Perhaps that's why he preferred the more good looking ones. He knew and relished this predilection even though he didn't understand it.

He looked into the face of the attractive Irina and his fingers tightened around her wrist. He could see the pain in her eyes and he wanted to see more.

"Friends!" he hissed. "Your kind has no friends - only clients." Just as suddenly he released her and leaned back in his seat. "Why pretend, comrade. We both know what you are and how it is that you can afford such clothes." He leaned forward and touched her knee. Her heavy winter coat, having been unbuttoned when she entered the compartment, had fallen open and exposed a silky looking dress beneath. Petrov rubbed the material of the dress as though if appreciating the quality of it. His touch this time was soft and gentle and he allowed his hand to stray slightly along her thigh. "Nice material - a very expensive dress. Must have cost you quite a few roubles."

Irina didn't mind his touching her like that so much because she realised that this was not the sort of man who would take any sexual advantage of her. He liked to hurt. She had come across men like Petrov before. They never wanted to enjoy women in the normal way. They just wanted to hurt. The more attractive the woman the more pain they would inflict. It was like a kind of jealousy. In some way she had to encourage him but she was beginning to appreciate that this man was likely to do anything. If he turned violent he could quite easily kill her - kill them all. Even together they would be no match for him. While he was stroking her leg she quickly glanced at the others. The small, shabby man next to her was watching with a sort of amused interest, while the luckless Olga was now sufficiently recovered to begin picking up her bits and pieces and reverently placing them in her bag. She didn't seem to be interested in anything else. The student and the young girl were trying hard not to look but were inevitably drawn to this new drama, which was now being played. There was nothing they could do or wanted to do - not until all of them had undergone the same treatment.

Petrov took his hand away and pursed his lips as he tried to make up his mind what was to be his next course of action. For a few minutes nothing was said. When it came it took everybody by surprise.

Without warning he suddenly swung a savage blow at Irina. The huge clenched fist exploded on the side of her face with the force of a sledgehammer and with the same effect. It might have been worse had she not been expecting some kind of spontaneous outburst like this, for she was already moving out of the way as the blow landed. Even so a blow delivered by a powerful man like Petrov, even when expected and partly avoided, was bound to damage and hurt.

Irina was knocked sideways into the small man who tried ineffectually to support her and at the same time to protect her as best he could. He knew what such a thump could feel like and he sympathised.

Of the others, the girl with the baby gave a small gasp of surprise and the student shifted in his seat as if he would stand, but he didn't.

Olga paused long enough in the re-possession of her belongings also to register a small look of surprise at the sudden onslaught.

Petrov, with fist still clenched, just smiled. "Didn't expect that, I bet." He was pleased with himself. He liked to vary his approach to his customers and he hadn't hit an attractive woman for a long time. It felt good. "That'll spoil your looks. Won't be so easy now to get clients." He grinned but quickly replaced the grin with a dark scowl. "That will teach you not to play games with me. When I ask questions I want straight answers, not evasion and lies. Now," he said as he thumped a clenched fist into the other hand making a loud, menacing, slapping sound, "let's have no more evasions shall we. Just answer my questions and don't flutter those made-up eyes, pretending you don't understand. I know all about your kind." He narrowed his eyes. "Though I must say I am surprised to find someone like you travelling on this train and flaunting yourself so openly."

Irina wasn't quite recovered from the shock of the blow. Already an ugly red mark testified to the force and accuracy of Petrov's punch, and a slight swelling began to appear. Though her eyes misted for a moment with the pain, they also flashed sharply - a warning perhaps, but the policeman didn't notice. At first she thought that he might have cracked a bone in her face but after some tentative probing she assured herself that it would turn out to be no more than a nasty bruise. It still hurt though and so did her wrist. She had made a vow to herself that she would get even with this bullying policeman. Meanwhile, she must still keep up the pretence but resolved to do nothing to provoke another outburst. Though in fact, she did not know what she had said to provoke the attack in the first place. She must assume that Petrov was some kind of psychotic who was likely to lash out suddenly at a whim. It was going to be difficult for all of them. She could only hope that he would not use his gun. Nevertheless, she felt that she ought to say something, to make some reply, before her silence encouraged him to more violence. It was often the case, for she had seen such situations before. Silence is worse than lying, especially with a man like this Petrov. Words at least would occupy him and give him something on which to concentrate. So she just mumbled something unintelligible.

Petrov was not really bothered by what she said unless it fuelled his questions and gave him further opportunities to make her feel uncomfortable.

"Your clothes are expensive. In fact everything about you is expensive. You have some rich friends I daresay. You certainly have come a long way. Most prostitutes have to be content with a few oranges. Why aren't you? Eh?"

He put his face close to hers and for a moment she thought

he was going to hit her again. She instinctively flinched away from him. Her reaction seemed to please him for he smiled.

Petrov enjoyed this kind of power when, by a small, innocent movement he could create almost as much terror as he could by actual physical force. "You are no better than her." He pointed to the kneeling figure of Olga, who was still painstakingly packing her belongings back into her bag. She didn't acknowledge the reference to herself, seemingly lost in her own thoughts.

The policeman continued. "You are nothing but a cheap whore. Your fancy clothes and painted face don't fool me. Presents! Ha!" He frowned and curled his lips as his fingers twitched nervously.

Irina believed that he was working himself up into striking her again and she tried to prepare herself for the blow. It didn't come.

The screwed up gargoyle's face of Petrov suddenly relaxed, though it was no less frightening. He had another thought and pondered on it before speaking.

"It seems to me that you may be more than a common prostitute. A few oranges is one thing but expensive gifts, real expensive gifts," he glanced at her wristwatch as he said this, "and those clothes could not be earned from ordinary street walking. You must know some very rich men, important men, powerful men." He nodded appreciatively at his own reasoning, which prompted him to a new line of questioning which had just occurred to him, and one which might prove much more worthwhile than the harassment of a cheap prostitute. "Now, comrade," he said with a sudden change to a more soothing tone, "let us not lose our tempers."

Irina was puzzled. Apart from the irony of his remark, she had a feeling that this policeman was beginning to think along different lines. She could tolerate the idea of being accused of prostitution but what she felt he now had in mind was something different, and could be much more dangerous. It could also be dangerous for Petrov himself, if it was what she thought. She only hoped that he would not pursue such ideas.

Petrov had rarely had much opportunity to utilise his talents in realms other than the fringes of espionage and state security. His superiors had long since decided that his coarseness and brutality were much more suited to the less important areas, with the less savoury and often more insignificant characters who inhabited the shady world of spies. The shabby Petrushka was a good example. Now, in the form of this attractive looking harlot whose expensive trappings were a clear sign that she must know some powerful people, he had a chance to break into the big time of his profession. He knew all about state secrets and prostitutes. It was common practice in some quarters and he was well aware that it was a method much used by his department, though mostly upon foreign officials and businessmen. He was just as sure that they would not use such a method against their own people. Or would they?

"Who are these friends of yours?" he asked pleasantly. "I don't suppose you have them long enough to even find out their names. Can you remember their names?" He tried to make his question sound casual, almost indifferent to the answer.

Irina did not reply. She did not know what to reply, because even if she invented names he was sure to see through any falsehood. For the moment it was perhaps better to remain silent. It might have the effect of egging him on and make him think that she knew more. She could only hope that his delight in his own cleverness would be enough to keep him asking the right questions, right that is from her point of view.

Petrov continued, still in his pleasant manner. "Where do you meet such people? They must be very wealthy and very important." He looked hard at her but seeing no reaction to this line of questioning he began to get annoyed. It was very easy for Petrov to become upset. He liked to get his own way all the time and always believed that the accused had the answers or information he wanted. It never occurred to him that there were many times when his questions could never produce answers from the miserable victims he chose to persecute. Petrov's trail was littered with such casualties.

"You're not having much luck, Comrade Policeman." Petrushka suddenly spoke. "Perhaps you're losing your touch. You were never much of a ladies man were you?" He chuckled at the pleasure it gave him to know that the barb had found its mark.

The policeman said nothing and tried to ignore what the small man had said yet in his heart he knew it to be true. He had probably killed more women he had failed to persuade than he had men. Was it perhaps that they were so weak and he was so strong? He had never believed it was like that. They always seemed to be mocking him, laughing in his face even when he was hurting them to the point of death. It never made any difference. They would never give in to him. They were all the same. It was the same with this smug, painted face now in front of him, already blotched with the ugly evidence of his handiwork. He wanted to smash that face to pulp. He wanted to obliterate it from his memory.

"What did you have in mind?"

Irina's voice had the effect of suddenly soothing the inner rage, which was building up within Petrov and would soon have erupted.

"Ah, so we are going to be co-operative after all. I am glad - for your sake. It would have been a pity to have to spoil such a pretty face permanently. How then would you have been able to earn your living?" He sniggered in a strange schoolboy way but quickly resumed his more usual manner. "Well, I want to know who you have slept with; where they live; and what they do for a living," he snapped out officiously.

"That is quite a lot of information. I'm not sure that I could remember all the details. You must give me some time to think about it."

Irina sounded convincing in her uncertainty, so much so that Petrov was prepared to believe her.

"Write them down," he said suddenly. "I don't want this riff-raff to hear state business."

Irina was relieved. She had at least bought a little time to think of something, which would be acceptable to this man Petrov. If he thought that through his cleverness he had stumbled upon something more important than a group of petty criminals, perhaps he would leave them alone. She was wrong though.

Petrov had no bounds to his appetite. They were not yet half way through their journey. He would need something more to pass the time. As far as he was concerned the game was very much in progress and not over by a long way.

"Do you have paper and a pen? I don't carry such things," Irina said half fearfully, for she could no longer guess what the policeman's reaction would be to even the most casual or innocent remark.

Petrov glowered. For a moment he suspected that it was another trick on the part of this over-priced whore but he reasoned with himself that it was not likely that she would have such items. She knew well enough that he could smash her face in if he wanted to and wouldn't risk lying to him. Of course he could always search her. He would enjoy that. He decided against it and instead he fumbled inside his heavy coat and produced the necessary items and handed them to her. "Here," he said gruffly, "and no tricks."

She took the paper and pen and after a short pause began to scribble something as Petrov watched intently. For the moment at least he was concerned only with the information that she could provide and would not be bothered with the others.

While Irina was writing the train rattled on through the night. It was still dark with dawn several hours away. No one really bothered to look at the changing panorama outside. There were fewer trees to obscure the white expanses of snow, which lay heavy on the ground and reflected back the light from the passing carriages.

If she had cared to look closely, the square faced Olga could perhaps have seen something of the passing countryside, but she was no longer interested. She had by now gathered up all her belongings and was back in her corner seat with her bag once more clutched tightly to her. This time she was staring ahead, brooding on the recent humiliation she had endured. Her grief was mostly for the lost roubles. She now contemplated with some gloom the possible fate, which awaited her when they reached Moscow.

As she scribbled, Irina began to think about the possible consequences of this action. The names and positions she was revealing were authentic for she did know many people of the type this policeman desired. How well she had known them was for him to guess at. He would probably be quite satisfied with this information. She knew it was no use trying to deceive him with false names. He could easily check. Her only problem was how to forewarn these people that this policeman would be investigating them. She knew that even if one of them were approached it would spell doom for her. She was in a difficult situation and until she could think of a way out of it she had to play along with Petrov.

At length she finished her writing and handed paper and pen to Petrov. He glanced at it and nodded appreciatively.

"Good. We shall see how accurate and honest you have been when we reach Moscow." He slipped the paper into the pocket of his coat where it now provided company for the roubles of Olga. He smiled and reached out and took Irina's face in one hand. He had large hands and when he squeezed her cheeks together so that her lips were distorted, she could not help but wince. "Now wasn't that easy. You and I will work together very well but of course you will understand that there will be no expensive gifts from me." He released her face and laughed aloud. It was a triumphant laugh for now he had broken the second person.

Irina slumped back in her seat fighting to hold back the anger and the humiliation she felt. Her face was red with shame and bruising, but her blue eyes shone with a cold intensity. She now knew with a cold certainty what she must do must do.

"Bravo, Comrade Policeman." The small, shabby man, Petrushka accompanied his words of praise with a loud clapping. It was a slow deliberate sound, which broke the silent lull. "You have conquered again. How easy it is for you. You must reveal to me how you can have such powers of persuasion. They are truly remarkable."

Petrov's annoyance with his prisoner was not apparent in his look, which was cold and impassive. Nevertheless it was there. Petrov was unsure about this man. He could not damage him too much because his superiors wanted him for extensive questioning. At the same time he could not let this clown continue with his sarcasm and mockery. Maybe he should beat him, but it did not seem to matter to this fool. He had already beaten him a couple of times but here he was, still shooting off his mouth. He would have to think of something special. He soon dismissed 'the clown' from his mind as he began to contemplate the two remaining passengers in the compartment. Which next he wondered - the young girl or the student? There was still plenty of time. He would choose the student. He rather relished the idea of keeping the young girl till last. It was surprising that he had heard nothing from that baby she hugged so close to her. Usually babies make such a row, sooner or later. He had thought about the possibility of shutting it up should it start howling. So far it had made no noise. He would have fun finding out more later. Meanwhile he began to turn his mind to the young man in the corner. "You!" he suddenly barked. "What is your name?"

The student looked up apprehensively. He knew that his turn had come.

Chapter Ten
Third Accusation

Mikhail Ivanov was not the student's real name, not altogether that is. He had 'borrowed' the surname of a friend just in case. His friends back in Leningrad had already made him aware that it was better not to travel under one's own name. If anything went wrong, it would help to confuse the authorities and allow time to cover up. He knew, therefore, that there was some element of danger involved in such a journey but he never expected that he would be accosted by a secret policeman so early or by chance. But was it by chance?

Mikhail had already witnessed two interrogations and realised that, though it might be no more than a bit of fun to the policeman, it could turn at any moment into something much more terrifying for the passengers. He had a strong suspicion that this man was close to being psychotic and might be capable of doing anything. He was also aware that without a weapon of any kind between them, they could do nothing to prevent him from continuing with his game. His very size was daunting enough and those hands of his could either squeeze the life out of him or mash him to pulp depending on how he felt. The young student had decided his own particular strategy as he had watched the two women being subjected to the policeman's torments. He didn't mind too much a certain amount of violence or coercion providing he could hold onto his secret. Would he have the cunning or the strength to outwit this bully? It remained to be seen. He swallowed nervously before replying to the policeman's question.

"Mikhail Ivanov," he said quietly and calmly, trying hard not to antagonise the questioner by inflection of tone or stress of his words.

"And what are you doing on this train, Comrade Student? You are a student are you not?"

The young student nodded. "Yes. I am a student and I am travelling to Moscow to see some friends." So far so good he thought.

Petrov was silent for a few moments. It was always his way when questioning suspects. He asked one or two insignificant or unimportant questions and then he waited. He would then study his subject to see if there was any reaction. Sometimes they showed too much relief or became too anxious. Whatever the question he asked, he only had to wait for them to show some sign of nervousness. He never took into consideration that any such anxiety displayed by his suspects might be directly caused by his own overbearing and menacing presence.

"You are studying at the university in Leningrad?"

The student nodded.

"What are you studying? Medicine? Biology? Economics? Sociology? Political Science?" Petrov rattled off the subjects so quickly that the student had barely time to make out what he was saying.

"I am studying Literature and History." Again he spoke calmly and carefully, trying hard not to lay undue emphasis on what he said. Already though he felt that the big policeman had decided his crime and was beginning to work his way towards it. If only he knew in advance of what he was suspected it might give him some chance at least to prepare his defence.

"What else do you do at your university? Seduce girls or take drugs? Or perhaps you write sedition? Have you ever been involved in any student demonstrations?" Petrov was still firing his questions rapidly one after the other.

"No. I don't do any of those things," the student replied,

and for the first time allowed some indignation to show in his voice. It was a mistake. He had fully accepted the fact that as far as Petrov the policeman was concerned, he was already guilty of something. To say otherwise or to express any kind of denial only encouraged him in his pursuit.

"What do you do then?" Petrov asked, and for the first time revealed silkiness in his tone which somehow exuded more menace than any of his earlier threats.

Mikhail the student was not quite sure what to answer for he sensed a trap in those words and the way they were spoken. He looked at Petrov and saw the flicker of a smile cross those stone-like features. He didn't know why but suddenly he felt very afraid of this big policeman.

"I...I don't know quite what you mean," he stammered.

"Don't be so coy. A healthy young man like you must have some sort of fun. It's only natural. You can't be expected to cram your head with all that knowledge and not want to burst out sometimes." Petrov spoke slowly, almost soothingly, and laid extra emphasis on the word 'knowledge'.

The student could not grasp the deeper meaning behind these questions for as yet he could not see that they were leading anywhere. Of course, Mikhail was young, very young and inexperienced in the ways of the world. Although a student once, he could not hope to understand the kind of world, which the sinister Petrov patrolled with relentless vigilance. Nor could he understand that, out there in the blackness rushing past the windows of the carriage, lay countless human beings of so much variety that it would make his head spin to comprehend.

Petrov knew and understood all types of people, however, and he had reduced them into two categories - guilty and innocent. He preferred the guilty because they were so much more interesting and their secrets were so much more interesting. He hadn't quite made up his mind what sort of crime this student had committed. He was still exploring various possibilities. With some gentle but persistent questioning he may be able to hint at a variety of crimes. He would try and gain his confidence. That sometimes worked, especially with young, impressionable men, who thought that they had ideals. Ideals usually covered up something sordid anyway. "Do you have any girl friends?" the policeman asked pleasantly.

The young student paused in his answer, only momentarily but long enough for Petrov to narrow his eye. "Yes," he said slowly, "but nobody regular you understand."

Petrov nodded. "I understand. You like girls but not all the time," he added slowly.

"I suppose so," the student muttered, not quite sure what the policeman meant by his remark.

It was Petrov's turn to pause as he considered his next question.

Meanwhile the student just waited passively still trying to convey a calm, unruffled manner.

"You have many friends?" the policeman asked innocently.

"I suppose I have really. I'm going to meet some of them in Moscow. That's why I'm going there." The student needn't have volunteered the extra information, but he felt that it might ease the situation and make his answers seem more natural. Perhaps it might help to convince the policeman that he had nothing to hide. Then he looked past Petrov and caught sight of the small man shaking his head slightly. He wondered what he meant by the gesture especially as it had been directed at him. Suddenly he was worried. He didn't think that he had said anything incriminating but it was difficult to tell with a man like Petrov. Mikhail decided to ignore the warning, if that's what it was. The other three didn't seem particularly bothered. The square faced woman was still staring into space and the attractive one was lost in her own thoughts.

"One of your girl friends perhaps?" Petrov added with a chuckle, "someone your parents don't approve of so you have to meet her out of town eh?" He almost whispered the last few words, as though it was just men's talk and shouldn't be overheard by the female passengers.

The student smiled and shook his head, unaware of the

trap, which had been laid for him. "Oh no. Nothing like that."

"Oh!" Petrov feigned surprise for a moment then in the same confidential tone as before he continued. "Ah I see. You expect to pick up a girl when you get to Moscow. I know you young students." He almost chuckled again.

"No...no," the student stammered slightly. "You don't understand."

"Oh I think I do. I understand very well, my young comrade." Petrov suddenly sounded severe and threatening but like a surprised teacher or parent. Then he relaxed again into his friendly and confidential manner. "Yes. Yes of course. You don't really care much for girls. Is that it? Why should that be? Can you tell me?"

Mikhail the student didn't know what to say. It seemed that this Petrov was going to twist any words he might speak into another meaning entirely. "No. I think you have mistaken me. I am not hoping to pick up a girl or anything like that. I'm just going to Moscow to meet with some friends. That's all.'

It wasn't all though, and Mikhail was sure the policeman had already guessed as much.

Petrov, however, chose to read other meanings into these protestations. "These friends are - boys, students like yourself?"

Mikhail nodded.

"Perhaps the truth of it, the real truth, is that you prefer boys to girls. Eh?" He spoke slowly so that the full weight of his meaning would not be lost on the student.

Mikhail had seen too late where the policeman's questions were taking him and he wanted to make some protest, a denial, but all he could say was a flustered 'no'. It was not enough. He knew it was not enough and all at once he found himself on the defensive about an accusation, which was wholly without foundation. He could not believe that such simple statements and answers could be so misunderstood or twisted that this Petrov now saw him as some sort of pervert. The idea revolted him but more than that was the fact that this secret policeman would regard it as the truth. He shifted uncomfortably on the seat for he now realised what the small, shabby man had been trying to say to him. He could feel himself getting warm and he started to sweat. A sure sign of guilt the policeman would say, but it was not true, none of it. He tried desperately to think of a suitable reply. By the leering look on the policeman's face he knew that there was no way he was going to convince him. It also occurred to him that very likely Petrov wanted it this way. He had already seen how he scared women and how, in contrast to the treatment meted out to them, his own treatment had been very gentle and soothing. He shuddered as the thought passed through his mind. Neither was he much relieved by the strange smile, which Petrov gave him.

"I'm not surprised by anything you students get up to. After all that search for knowledge eh?" Petrov sounded tolerant, even genial. "I understand my boy. I understand." He patted the student on his knee in a paternal fashion - or it might have meant something else.

The young student wanted to flinch at the touch, but didn't. That also worried him.

"Some people, I don't say that I am one of them, would frown on such behaviour. But times are changing and I suppose we must change with them."

Petrov sounded so friendly that the young man grew more uncertain and ill at ease. He knew very well what this policeman was capable of doing. He had already been an unwilling witness to his savage outbursts, or did he reserve such treatment only for females? No, of course not. That small man had been beaten. Mikhail wished in a way that he had been more roughly treated. He couldn't bear this soft, friendly, fatherly approach, if it was a fatherly approach. He was by now totally confused and always when he looked at Petrov he saw him smiling in that strange way as if they both shared a very special secret. He tried once more to express some sort of denial but not very effectively. "I think you have misunderstood when I mentioned my friends in Moscow. There is a girl there who I know quite well." He paused and rubbed his hands nervously. "I slept with her once," he suddenly blurted out.

If he thought such a statement would alter the line of questioning by the policeman, he was wrong. All it produced was an understanding nod and an affected sigh from Petrov.

"You have to keep up appearances. I see that. It must be very difficult for you, being different from your other friends." He paused, "or perhaps they have similar tastes to your own."

Mikhail didn't know whether Petrov wanted a reply or not, but resolved to volunteer no further information unless specifically requested.

"I envy you students. We secret policeman lead such dull lives by comparison. I'm sure that you get up to all sorts of things - out of school, so to speak. What about parties then?"

Petrov had taken his time in getting to the real accusation he had decided upon. He had already made this young student nervous and very uncomfortable without once threatening or even hinting at any kind of force or duress. He had merely made a suggestion and let the young man fill in the details. Soon he would make his swoop but not just yet. He was enjoying himself. He rather liked the friendly approach and made a mental note to use it more often, particularly on those susceptible young males, who came within his sphere of influence. He would never try it with females.

"Parties?" Mikhail was confused again. He found it bewildering to try and keep up with the exact line of this policeman's questioning. In one way the questions seemed quite random and innocent and yet he was never quite sure. The friendlier Petrov became the more afraid the young student became.

Petrov nodded encouragingly. "Yes - those orgies that we hear so much about. Oh I know that they're not supposed to happen in this country, but we in the department get to hear about them." He smiled broadly, like one who was perhaps expecting to be invited to such a party on the strength of his short acquaintance with the student.

This made Mikhail wary. Was he genuinely interested in such things as a policeman or did he want to know for himself? He was unsure. From the strange looks and friendly attitude already conveyed in this interview, for it could not really be called an interrogation, he could well believe that this huge frightening person had other interests and cravings.

"I don't know much about those sort of things, I have never been to one. I have never even heard of one taking place I..." Mikhail was about to continue but then he remembered. It was best not to say too much. He hoped that he had learnt that much.

"A pity, I had hoped that you would tell me something about what goes on at such meetings. Someone like me, specially being a policeman, would never have such an opportunity of seeing how the young people take their pleasures." Petrov sounded as though he had abandoned that line of enquiry.

The relief must have shown on the student's face. Although Petrov misconstrued that look of relief, it did lead him to go back to his earlier insinuation.

"Of course, I was forgetting. Such parties would mean girls. They wouldn't be of much interest to you would they? Do you spend much time at your studies?"

The abrupt change of subject caught Mikhail off guard and before he realised it he was confiding details of his work schedules and hours of study. He felt a certain pride in trying to impress with the depth of his learning even though he was sure that Petrov was not really appreciative. He began to regret that he had given all that up though he could not confide as much to his questioner.

"Do you work alone much?"

"Most of the time."

"But with friends as well, perhaps with a special friend. Tell me about him, this special friend of yours. Is he a student like you? Or perhaps he is a lecturer." Petrov pushed the questions at Mikhail quickly one after the other. He knew that he was on the point of breaking him although the young student didn't know it. "What is he like, this special friend of yours? I am interested in what young, healthy men like yourself get up to, that is if they don't have girl friends."

The young student was completely flustered. Again he wanted to protest that it wasn't like that. "I don't have any friends - well yes I do but no one particular friend." He saw that the policeman was looking at him in a way that showed he didn't believe him. He hastily tried to explain further. "I am no different to any other student I suppose."

"Oh but you are, Mikhail." Petrov used the student's first name and that sent a cold shiver down the young man's spine. "We both know that you are different," he nodded in affirmation that it was so. "We understand such things. I don't blame you." Petrov continued to speak reassuringly and softly. Once more, to emphasise his friendliness and fatherly approach he laid his hand on the student's knee and gave it a slight squeeze.

Mikhail was a mixture of emotions. This policeman had deliberately twisted his most innocent statements and nothing he could now say seemed to make the slightest difference or persuade him otherwise. He was terribly confused. Though he was not sure what this sinister man wanted, somewhere at the back of his mind he sensed that it might not be for anything he had done but for what Petrov believed him to be. He remembered again the violence, which he had used towards the attractive woman passenger, and this made him wonder. Could there be more than one side to this brutal policeman? It also made him ask questions about himself. It made him uncertain. Always before he had been so sure but now, perhaps for the first and only time in his life, another man was suggesting strange, impossible things about him and yet the tone and manner of the suggestions made it all seem so likely. Furthermore, he was still concerned that the policeman was trying to find out something more about him and his friends. He knew in his heart that he could really tell him little more than he had so far admitted. Yet always the questions were there. Whichever way he faced he felt himself slowly but surely being squeezed till he knew that there would come a moment when he would tell Petrov anything he wanted to know, whether it was the truth or not. In an odd sort of way he felt that he should somehow repay the friendliness and tolerance shown towards him by the policeman, yet he didn't know how he could do that. He looked around at the others. They were taking no notice of his predicament. Not even the small shabby man, known as Petrushka, seemed to be interested. He needed guidance - help - something. He was afraid of this policeman but he could not identify the exact nature of his fear. It seemed to be bound up with so many other things. He just wished to be left alone.

"I..." Mikhail began, wanting to say something but finding that he couldn't properly express his thoughts.

"You want to say something?" Petrov asked gently. "You can tell me, not as a policeman but as a friend, a close friend." He leaned closer and spoke in a low voice. "Women don't really understand such friendships - what one man can feel for another. What do they know of comradeship or loyalty? Nothing. It's up to you and me to show them what real trust is." He paused for a moment and looked hard at the student. "I trust you. You can surely trust me." He paused again. "I haven't done anything to hurt you, have I?"

The student shook his head glumly.

"Nor will I. But just between us men, tell me what your friends - your other friends that is - are like."

"Not much to tell really," Mikhail said quietly. "Just like me I suppose. We're nothing special although we like to think we are. We meet after studies sometimes and talk and smoke, or maybe a drink. Nothing much."

"You enjoy being with your friends?"

"Yes of course. It's good to relax with friends after studying."

"They are your special friends." Petrov put added emphasis on the word 'special'.

It should have warned the student to beware but he didn't notice or perhaps by now he didn't care.

"Yes. I suppose they are my special friends. Nothing wrong in having special friends is there?"

Petrov beamed in his usual toothy way. "That's what I've

been saying, Mikhail, all along."

Mikhail also smiled but it was a small, forced smile. He felt less threatened by Petrov and he also felt more at ease in talking to him.

"Would you say that we are special friends?" Petrov had now baited the hook and it only remained for the young student to take the bait.

Unable to answer anything else, Mikhail nodded and mumbled 'yes'.

Petrov was pleased but his look became serious yet not threatening. He suddenly extended his arm and held out his hand. "Let me have the drugs Mikhail. They will be safer with me."

Mikhail was not surprised. He knew in his heart that it was coming to this. There was not much further point in holding out. Had he been more prepared he might have lasted a little longer. Who could say? Without another word he took some small packets from an inside pocket of his coat and put them into the large waiting hand.

"I know that is all you have for you would not deceive a friend would you?" Petrov spoke soberly and softly, without malice or threat. But then he didn't need to. He had completely mastered the young student.

Mikhail nodded. "No deceptions. That's all. I promise."

"I believe you. We will say no more." Petrov took the small packets and without even examining them slipped them into the same voluminous pocket, which already housed Olga's roubles and Irina's notes.

"Now that was clever." Petrushka suddenly spoke up. "I applaud you, Comrade Petrov. You were masterly." He then proceeded to clap but with less mockery than before. When he stopped he shook his head in some disbelief at what he had witnessed, and accompanied it with a slight incredulous smile. "You know, comrade, you really are very good. I mean it."

Petrov the policeman eyed the small, shabby man with a dark, suspicious look and for a moment it seemed that he might offer a reply. Instead he just waved a hand in dismissal of such praise as not being worthy coming from someone like Petrushka. Petrov didn't trust his prisoner one little bit and was quite sure that any remark was calculated to either annoy him or throw him off his guard.

"Of course," Petrushka added slyly, "he was only a boy."

"What do you mean by that?" Petrov asked with a touch more of his usual threatening tone in his voice.

"Nothing - nothing," the small man replied innocently. "It just occurred to me that your tactics might not have been so successful with a grown man. With a grown man it would have to have been force."

"You are right comrade, it would have been force. Now shut your mouth or I will demonstrate the art of force."

Once more the small compartment was plunged into silence, a silence, which was still heavy and oppressive. Each traveller knew that there was still much more to come. They sat with their own thoughts while the gentle, metallic rattle of the wheels of the train ticked off the minutes till dawn as well as the miles to Moscow.

It was now somewhere near three-thirty in the early part of the morning. Outside it was still dark with the temperature below zero. If any of the passengers had cared to look through the windows they might possibly have discerned that the expanses of snow-covered fields were now not so much in evidence for they were passing through areas of dense pine forests. It is more than likely that the five of them could at least have wished themselves somewhere out among the tall, gaunt trees and tramping through the last of the winter snows rather than be inside here in the claustrophobic warmth with the policeman Petrov.

Suddenly the young girl stood up and hesitatingly tried to open the door. With her baby still clutched tightly in her arms this was proving to be a problem she would not easily solve. "I need to go to the end of the corridor," she said by way of explanation. She looked first at Petrov and then around at the others. They all then looked at the policeman, who didn't seem to be concerned one way or the other.

The young student Mikhail, awaking from his reverie, suddenly became aware or the young girl's predicament. He stood up and slid back the door of the compartment.

The young girl, with a nervous glance behind her, slipped out into the corridor.

If the others had thought that Petrov was no longer interested in the girl, they were mistaken. It didn't matter to him that she had temporarily slipped from his clutches. He had already ascertained from the conductress that the communicating door between the carriages was now locked and could only be opened on her authority. Apparently such precautions were necessary to prevent the tourists from wandering about and mixing with ordinary Russian travellers. At least that's what Petrov surmised, and he was probably right. He smiled to himself at the thought. So he knew that she would be back soon enough even if she tried to remain in the corridor for the rest of the journey. He had given his own instructions to the conductress and at the same time had made it clear that it were best that she pay heed to them.

He leaned back and waited. It would give him time to think of something for the girl, and her baby. His thoughts lingered on the baby. It had made no sound and no movement either, not that he had noticed. The more he thought about her, the more his idea was shaping into a definite accusation.

By a coincidence he had just made up his mind when the compartment door was slid back and the young girl with her baby slipped back inside. She still looked nervous and glanced anxiously around the compartment as if seeking a friendly face. The disappointment in her eyes was plain to see, for none of her fellow passengers seemed to have any interest in her plight. She also knew that, despite the silence and apparent acquiescence of the policeman in letting her leave, he had not forgotten her and would resume his cruel game when it should suit him.

Petrov looked at her. It was not a look, which showed any particular emotion. Indeed it might have been better if he had displayed some sort of physical sign. Instead he just looked at her as if he were reading a book. This only made her more nervous than she was, if that was possible.

At length the policeman spoke, startling the others into half attention. They had almost been lulled into thinking that he would not bother with the girl after the previous interview. They were wrong but not altogether surprised.

"Now it is your turn. Did you think that I might overlook you, or your baby? Let's talk about your baby, shall we?"

As his deep ominous tones assailed her ears, the young girl, Natalia trembled and shivered all at once. What she had most feared, even before the journey had begun, and the policeman had entered their compartment, was now about to happen. Wherever she was, she knew that her turn would come sooner or later. Now it was here.

Chapter Eleven
The Final Accusation

Olga had once more resumed her pastime of looking out of the window, though now she did it mechanically and without any kind of enthusiasm. Maybe it was the vague suspicion of dawn creeping over the horizon and throwing the tall trees into a sharper, more definite relief, which had mesmerised her. It was difficult to tell. Dawn was still an hour or so away and poor Olga had not really noticed much since her 'breakdown'. Whether it was a total breakdown could not be determined with a woman like her. Whatever had been taken from her had been the source of her hope. It didn't seem likely that she would recover.

The policeman Petrov could also discern that the darkness outside had become softer and that dawn could not be too far away. But he still had plenty of time. In any case they were not due in Moscow for another three hours or so. There was plenty of time. Had he forgotten that they also stopped at Kalinin, which was only half an hour distant? Probably not - Petrov appeared to be the kind of person who took everything into account. It was also beginning to look as though he knew everything. He certainly knew about people and their weaknesses. With the young girl it was going to be too easy. He knew too much about her. He could write her entire life story just by looking at her. Still, he would spin it out as much as he could. Who knows? If he played the game properly he might easily encourage one or two of the others to join in. He glanced quickly around at them. He could never take things for granted. Although they each looked subdued, he couldn't really tell how they might react. Not for sure. The only one he was sure of was that pathetic creature, Petrushka. He wouldn't interfere, except with his clever remarks. He was nothing. As for the rest - they looked as though they had nothing more to live for. That was close to the truth he thought, especially if he had his way with them. Thus he dismissed them from his mind - for the moment. He turned again to the young girl.

"What's the baby's name?" He asked politely enough as any interested passer-by might enquire of a proud mother.

Natalia had waited a long time for this moment. Though it was what she had dreaded, now it was here she felt a strange kind of relief. But that relief did not automatically cancel out the terrible fear of what she felt was going to happen to her and her baby.

"He doesn't have a name - yet," she replied, with as much bravado as she could manage. She must not let him see that she is afraid, she reasoned with herself. That would only make him angry and then he would do terrible things to her like he did to the other woman. So she sat and waited patiently for more questions to come.

"You have a name though?"

Natalia nodded but said nothing. She had decided to say nothing unless she was asked a direct question.

"Well? What is your name?" Petrov asked without seeming annoyed at the reluctance of the young girl.

"Natalia," she whispered.

"Where is the baby's father, Natalia? The baby has no name. Why does it have no name? Is it not worth giving a name to?" He reeled off the questions rapidly, giving her no time to think or answer any of them. It was his usual trick when he wanted to confuse and fluster his victim. He didn't have to try too hard with the young girl for she was flustered to begin with. "Well? Are you going to answer me or do I have to think the worst?" Petrov adopted a sterner, more insistent manner.

The young girl just stared wildly in front of her trying to think what to say, but though her mouth moved no sounds came out of it.

"Take your time," the policeman said soothingly. "Just answer one question at a time. Now Natalia," he said slowly, "where is the baby's father?"

"In Leningrad. He's in Leningrad," she stammered uncertainly. "He's in Leningrad...Leningrad," she repeated several times, slowly and quietly to herself.

"So he's in Leningrad. Why does he not travel with you and the baby?"

The young girl looked at Petrov as if to suggest it was a foolish question, to which he ought to know the answer. That look should also have been a warning to him that the girl Natalia was not altogether capable of giving him the answers he expected or wanted.

"Why should he travel with me and my baby? There's no rule to say that he must travel with us is there?" She replied in a mixture of annoyance and concern as the various possibilities posed by the policeman's questions occurred to her.

For the first time in his interrogation Petrov was nonplussed. He paused to consider carefully what he should next ask her. He understood well enough the fact that women with young babies were apt to be over protective and extra cautious in all their dealings with strangers. But already the behaviour of this young girl was not following the usual pattern. The only time he had come across such an attitude to his questions was when he had to deal with political suspects who had undergone certain types of surgery. She was like one of them, not in the same world as the rest of them, but sharp enough, however, to pick out the more subtle aspects of his 'interview'. But then it only strengthened his conviction that he knew her crime and her behaviour was, and had been all along, quite natural in the circumstances. Perhaps he would play along with her for a little while yet before he confronted her with the big question. It would give him some added amusement.

"Why does your husband not travel with you?" he asked gently.

Natalia thought for a moment. "He can't. He's working. He has an important job in Leningrad and can't spare the time. That's it. He can't spare the time." She seemed pleased with her answer and for a brief moment her face almost broke into a self-congratulatory smile. But it quickly disappeared to be replaced by the same hollow-eyed stare with which she had entered the compartment at the beginning of the journey.

Petrov was about to ask her another question when he was interrupted by a wheezing chuckle. It came from the small, shabby man, and as before it contained a certain amount of mockery at the attempt of the policeman to interrogate his subjects.

"You will have your work cut out with that one, comrade. If you can't see it the rest of us can." He chuckled again and shook his head in accompaniment to his words.

"You shut up." Petrov snarled and stretched out a warning finger, "or it'll be the worse for you."

The small, shabby did shut up, but the lingering smirk on his face betrayed the inner joy he felt at what he thought to be a difficult task for the policeman.

"What is your husband's name?" Again Petrov put his question as gently as he could. He had already decided that it was not the words themselves that would have the greatest effect with the young girl but the manner in which he spoke them.

Natalia said nothing for a while then, as if triggered by some inner thought, she replied calmly and without emotion, "Boris. His name is Boris. My husband is called Boris but we have not yet given the baby a name."

"I know that," said Petrov patiently. "Your husband's name is Boris but your baby does not yet have a name." He paused. "Is Boris the father of your baby?"

For a moment it seemed that the young girl was not going to answer. Her eyes began to fill with tears but the expression on her face did not alter.

"Yes. He is," she whispered at length.

"Do you want to tell me about Boris?"

She shook her head and closed her lips tight.

"Perhaps you have had a quarrel with him and now you are running away. That's it, isn't it?"

The young girl shook her head. "I'm going to Moscow. I am going to stay with my aunt. My aunt lives in Moscow. She will look after me."

She spoke her sentences in a jerky, staccato manner, like one who is making up her answers as she thinks of them, or like a child who has only a certain number of fixed responses in her head and trundles them out in order of importance. "Yes, I am going to Moscow," she repeated before Petrov could get in another question. "My aunt will look after me - she will look after me."

The strange and somewhat haphazard replies from the young girl had begun at last to arouse the interest of the others, and one by one they became increasingly intrigued by her. The same question went through all their minds. What would Petrov do next? How long would he tolerate this childlike prattle? For that's what it was becoming.

Irina knew to her cost that he would have no qualms in striking her if she continued to exhibit such affected childishness, for she knew that it was just that.

The attractive Irina, like the others, had not yet, however, come to terms with the fact that this policeman Petrov, ugly and brutal though he may be, was possibly a very clever man. They should have learned by now that he had a technique to suit every occasion and every suspect. The only handicap under which he suffered was lack of time. The blackness outside the train was not so intense and it wanted only another fifteen minutes before the first stop at Kalinin. It was unlikely that there would be anyone boarding the train at that hour, thus possibly interrupting his interrogation. But Petrov did not want to take any chances now he was so close. Nevertheless, he was becoming more conscious of the time factor though it flattered his ego to think that he could break this young girl any time he liked. The more she spoke, the more he was certain of the exact nature of her transgression.

"What's your aunt's name?"

"I don't know. Natalia something I think." She screwed up her eyes as if trying to remember but then shook her head in acknowledgement that the effort defeated her.

"But that's your name, isn't it?" Petrov looked confused for a moment.

"Yes. It's also my aunt's name. I was named after her. She is my favourite aunt."

"It's a long way to travel from Moscow to Leningrad. I should not like to think that my daughter was taking such a journey on her own."

Petrov had deliberately reversed the destinations and waited to see if the girl would respond.

"It is a long way. But I have my baby and Boris will meet me," she said simply. "We shall manage. My parents don't really care."

"But you said that Boris was in Leningrad. How then can he be waiting for you in Moscow?"

The young girl looked at the policeman, her face betraying no emotion. In her mind it was simple enough. Why didn't he understand? She was not running away from Boris at all. She was going to meet him. The train, these people, and the darkness outside made her nervous. That's all there was to it. She would be alright once the journey was over. She was certain. Why doesn't he ask more questions, she thought. He should ask more questions then she could tell him her answers and get it over with. He wouldn't hit her like he did that other woman, not while she had the baby. She must look after the baby. "Boris is waiting for me," she said simply and it looked as though that was all she was going to say.

Petrov felt that it was time now to probe deeper. Time was getting short and he could not afford to waste too much of it on this girl. He still had to decide what to do with the rest of them when he reached Moscow. How he wished for the old days. It would have been so much simpler just to shoot them and leave the railway people to clean up. They were no more than litter anyway.

He moved closer to the girl and made to touch the baby. Quickly she turned away and shrank into the corner of the seat.

"I wasn't going to hurt him. I only wanted to look."

The girl scowled and hugged the baby tighter, if that was possible. She had held it so close to her that surely she must have succeeded in suffocating it on several occasions since the start of the journey. It had remained remarkably quiet so far. "Please don't touch my baby. He's asleep."

Petrov nodded in understanding, or at least a pretended understanding. "I won't disturb him. I just wondered if he looked like Boris at all."

The girl shook her head. "Not like Boris," she murmured to herself and looked under the folds of the shawl as if to confirm her opinion.

Petrov leaned across slightly to see if she would relax and allow him to look at the baby. But again when he made such a movement she hastily pulled up the folds of the shawl and half turned away from him.

"So Boris is meeting you in Moscow," Petrov said pleasantly enough but then he dropped his polite manner. "But I thought you said he was in Leningrad," he suddenly rasped. It was time to adopt a harsher, more demanding tone.

The girl was startled and wasn't sure what to say.

Petrov saw her uncertainty and pressed his advantage.

"The truth is that you don't know where your precious Boris is. Shall I tell you why?"

"No - no. I don't want to hear you. No more questions. Please no more questions." The young girl was by now quite agitated at the thought of what the policeman was about to say. She began to get out of her seat but the strong hand of Petrov upon her arm forced her back down.

"You stay there, comrade and listen. There will be no more questions - just one maybe," he added slyly as an afterthought. "Yes, just one." He paused and pushed his face close to hers.

"Does this precious Boris of yours love you?" He lingered on the question and leered triumphantly as he waited for her reply.

Natalia didn't seem sure what to say. She nodded stiffly and without any conviction. "He loves me. I know he loves me." She repeated the phrase several times as though trying to burn it into her memory. "He is waiting for me," she added brightly and seemed to think that such information was sufficient for the enquiring Petrov.

The policeman continued to leer. "He doesn't love you. Why do you say he does? He left you months ago. He doesn't love you at all." He rammed these statements into her just as he would a dagger. They hurt just as much and he knew it. For Petrov it was only a prelude. He had to weaken with such thrusts till he could confront her with the real truth. "He doesn't love you," he repeated. "He never did love you. How could he love someone like you?" Petrov began to taunt her with the idea and it was beginning to have some effect.

Natalia was becoming more agitated and she began to twist and shift about on her seat. She wanted to get up but whenever she tried to get away from these lies, the policeman would pull her back down. She was trapped and helpless. The others weren't interested in her, she was sure of that. They thought she was crazy or something. She could tell by the looks on their faces.

"Boris doesn't love you. He never loved you." Petrov repeated the words, which seemed to have such an effect on the young girl. "He is not waiting for you in Moscow at all."

"He does love me. He does, he does," the young girl muttered through clenched teeth, still trying to make the words into fact, but she knew in her heart it was not true. If she stopped thinking that then everything will have been for nothing. She had to believe in Boris. He was the father of her child. Why will this policeman not believe her? How could she make him believe?

"You're not going to win with that one, Comrade Interrogator." The small, shabby man spoke up once more and tapped the side of his forehead to indicate that the girl was not quite right in the head.

"Are you some sort of doctor then?" Petrov muttered.

"No, but anyone can see that she is - mentally disturbed. She cannot answer your questions or respond in any way, even if she wanted to. She's deranged. It would be best to leave her alone."

Petrushka knew that he was probably pleading for the girl's life for if she did not yield to the bullying questions of the policeman he would summon up more physical persuasion. He knew that Petrov would do it, especially as time was running out.

"Go to sleep and keep your nose out of this. I know more than you think and don't need your advice," Petrov growled. "If you need any help getting to sleep let me know."

Petrushka said nothing and with a resigned shrug leaned his head back against the padded seat. He did not sleep or close his eyes but casually looked at the other passengers. They didn't seem too interested in what was going on, then why should they. Each of them had already suffered and been humiliated in their different ways. They were not used to such treatment. Not like him. He knew what it was like well enough. He was nevertheless intrigued at the range and versatility of this policeman. He did seem to know what he was doing. Petrushka smiled to himself. Of course it's easy when you're twice the size of an average person, and you carry a gun. It's even easier if you are not only trained to torture and kill, but that you actually enjoy doing it and look for ways to satisfy that lust. That's exactly how it is with Petrov. Petrushka yawned. He was tired and would like to have taken the policeman's advice but he felt that he ought to remain awake for the rest of the journey. He had a strong feeling that something surprising was going to happen and he wanted to be part of it.

Of the others, perhaps, only the attractive Irina felt the same as the shabby man on the seat next to her. After all, she had a special reason for thinking that. It would help if she could talk to the others, especially the man next to her. She realised though that it was virtually impossible with that policeman in the compartment. She had only half listened to what he was saying to the girl and, remembering what he had done to herself, she reckoned that it wouldn't be too long before he lost his temper and went back to brute force. The baby wouldn't stop him. She knew his kind only too well. He would break her soon. Irina was sure of it. If only she could think of something to get her out of this carriage and out of this situation. There was still a long way to go before they reached Moscow. She glanced at the square faced woman in the corner. She did not seem as graceless as before.

Olga in fact sat like a dead person and only very occasionally did her small, button shaped eyes glare at what else may be going on around her.

The student, Mikhail had completely withdrawn into himself. He held his head in his hands mostly and had looked at nobody since his own ordeal.

There was nothing Irina could do, therefore, except wait - and watch the continuing interrogation.

Not heeding in the slightest the advice proffered by the small, shabby man, Petrushka, Petrov continued with his questions. For the moment it was the same question.

"Are you so sure that Boris loves you?" he said quietly and softly. "Because if he did, he would be waiting for you in Moscow. Wouldn't he?" He nodded to the girl who, mesmerised by his words and gentleness of his tone, also nodded in acknowledgement. "He won't be waiting for you in Moscow because we both know that he lives in Leningrad, don't we?" He nodded again and she imitated him. "Why don't you admit the truth of it? Boris left you a long time ago. In fact you barely knew Boris. Isn't that the real truth?" The soft tones were gradually being replaced by stronger, more urgent demands. At each question the girl nodded in confirmation of the supposition put forward by the policeman.

Suddenly she burst out. "It's true. It's true. Boris lives in Leningrad. Somewhere in Leningrad but I don't know where.

He used to live in Moscow. That's where I met him. But now he lives in Leningrad and I can't find him." The tears, which had been threatening, slowly began to trickle down her face and yet she was oblivious to the fact that she was weeping, for her manner was still the same. With wide, staring eyes, from which her tears were bubbling, she turned to Petrov. "Boris doesn't love me, does he or he would have met me and my baby?"

Petrov grinned. That's it, he thought. It was too easy. "Now tell the truth of the matter," he suddenly snarled. There were to be no more soft words. Not now.

"The truth," she stammered. "What truth do you mean?"

"Yes, Comrade Unmarried Mother, the truth, if you know what such a thing is. Or shall I tell you the real truth of it?"

The young girl could only shake her head in a vague manner and murmur something inaudible. She wasn't sure that she knew the truth of it herself. She wasn't sure about anything, except her baby. That was the real truth.

"The real truth," Petrov hissed in her ear, "is that you are a slut. The real truth is that there is no Boris. You made him up once you found that you were pregnant. Oh it's better to have been deserted by a lover than to have had no lover at all. Isn't it, Comrade Slut?" Petrov would have achieved the same result had he decided to beat the girl, for she winced at each accusation, but didn't deny any of them. Nor was he finished. "The truth is that you live in Moscow and went to Leningrad to have your baby and perhaps at the same time trap some poor fool into acknowledging the fatherhood of the bastard. But you were not very successful were you? It was a waste of time."

"Having a baby is not a crime yet, Comrade Policeman, even if there is no father to give it a name." The small man Petrushka had spoken once again. "But then I suppose you would make it a crime just to make your game work out."

Petrov turned to his prisoner and smiled. "Jumping to conclusions again, comrade. However I regard this slut and her bastard, I have accused her of nothing. What she may have done and has attempted to conceal by making up fairy stories about it, is her business. But you don't know much about people do you?" He paused and looked at Petrushka thoughtfully. "You have watched me play my game with these people. You should have a good idea of how I operate by now, and how I am always right. Do you think that you could do any better comrade? Do you think that you could imagine the crime that this girl has committed? Are you that clever, Comrade Petrushka, known as the Clown?" Petrov looked hard at the small, shabby man and smirked. He was revelling in his own cleverness and now he had a chance to make this loud-mouth, know-all hold his tongue once and for all. He waited for the challenge to be taken up.

Petrushka was somewhat bemused at the challenge thrown out by the overbearing Petrov. He wasn't sure what he meant for a start. He looked into the ugly, grinning face and realised that the policeman meant exactly what he said. He then studied the girl, who was sitting on the edge of her seat and clutching the baby tightly as she had done all along. He felt sorry for her and anger at the brutal way Petrov had made her acknowledge her plight. But then Petrushka was sorry for all of them, even the brutal Petrov.

Whilst he had learned something unpleasant about his fellow travellers he had, through the course of the four interrogations, learned a great deal more about Petrov himself. The most important thing he had learned about him was that he was an extremely dangerous man whose highly charged and volatile nature could burst out and destroy them all at the slightest wrong move and at any moment. Could this be such a moment? Should he play this policeman's game, if only to keep him quiet? There was no question of choices, not to judge by the look on the policeman's face.

"Take your time, comrade. We have a little while before Kalinin. You should be able to manage it. You are the clever one. After all I am only a policeman." Petrov laughed out loud.

Petrushka looked at the others, who had suddenly begun to show some interest in the new turn of events. They all looked towards him, even the student, as though his pronouncement would somehow help to save them. He could only shake his head at the futility and stupidity of the idea. He looked across at the girl again and tried to imagine what crime she could possibly have committed. Petrov was sure that she had committed some crime and he hadn't been far wrong yet. She looked so forlorn, so pathetic. Why did she have to travel on this train? Why did she have to go to Leningrad at all? Was there no-one back home that could have helped her? He looked closely at her clothes. They were not the clothes of a real poor person. That didn't help much. Did she have any parents, he wondered?

"May I ask one question, Comrade Policeman?"

Petrov nodded. "Make it short and just one question,"

Petrushka leaned towards the girl. "Natalia," he said quietly, "tell me about your parents, your mother and your father,"

The young girl, hearing a new voice, turned in its direction, "My parents are dead. I live with my aunt in Moscow. That's where I'm going now – home." She spoke in a flat, unemotional way, like one who has come through a great ordeal and has been drained of strength and energy.

Petrushka noted this change and yet he could not believe that it was entirely as a result of the policeman's questions. To him it seemed that she had become reconciled to some fact in her life, past or present, but not a happy one. It worried him. He began to sense that perhaps this grinning policeman was right again. There was something more to find out but he could not fathom what it might be. For the sake of beating this policeman at his own game he could guess, but it would only be a guess. He had no way of knowing what secret was concealed behind those round dead eyes. In any case, he reasoned, if he should successfully guess her crime it would do none of them any good. To be right would only enrage Petrov and could spark off who knows what sort of trouble for them all. The best thing he could do was to admit defeat and let Petrov prove to them how clever he was.

He threw up his hands. "I could only make guesses,

Comrade Policeman, I don't have your peculiar gift of insight into the tormented souls of others but, for what it is worth, I think you are wrong. She is guilty of no crime, only of being young and foolish. I am sure that even you were like that once upon a time."

"You can't resist being clever can you Petrushka? But you admit defeat and you think I am wrong. Well I'm not. I have never been more right." He turned to the girl and then he turned back to Petrushka. "I have already uncovered several types of crime. You have witnessed it. I have proved what I believe about people. Everyone has something to hide, something against the state I mean, something serious." He paused and lowered his voice a fraction to lend emphasis to his next words. "Well? You can't get more serious than murder."

If the word 'murder' was introduced to create the necessary effect, Petrov couldn't have been more pleased at the result.

Even Olga, of the dour features shook her head in disbelief.

Petrushka laughed out loud.

The attractive Irina was sure that this policeman did not really expect them to believe such a thing. "I think you are crazy," she said coldly. "The things you have already accused the rest of us of are small things compared to murder and yet you claim that this poor child has...It's too ridiculous, even for you." She spoke with an air of certainty, like one who is in possession of all the facts.

The student didn't say anything but from the expression on his face it was clear that he didn't believe this accusation either.

The girl herself had said nothing nor made any exclamation. It was almost as if they were talking about someone else and not her at all.

Petrov looked at the four of them. He wanted to smile at their stupidity but would not allow himself to show any expression but one of contempt.

"You have such noble thoughts about your fellow men, and women. I don't. I see them - you - for what you are -

criminals against the state and the system. She is no different." He turned and pointed to the girl Natalia, who was still taking no notice of what was going on or being said about her. "And I will prove it." He edged closer to her and tried to look at the baby in her arms. As soon as she was aware of his presence and his intention she turned away almost facing the door.

"Your baby is still sleeping then?"

Natalia nodded.

"Does it not wake for food? We have been on this train for several hours now and it has not made one sound. Are you sure it is asleep?"

For a moment a look of fear flitted across the face of the young girl to be quickly replaced by a weak smile. She peered into the bundle in her arms but quickly covered up the baby as Petrov leaned across.

"It is unusual for a baby to be so quiet. Are you sure it is asleep?" He repeated the question but there was no mistaking his sinister inference.

"Babies need a lot of sleep. Everyone knows that."

Surprisingly it was Olga, the square faced woman, who suddenly spoke up but then didn't seem inclined to say any more.

"I'm very worried about this baby," Petrov continued and ignored the previous remark. "It has slept too long. Perhaps it is ill. I think we ought to look at it and make sure. I'm sure these other women will know what to do."

"No! No! You can't touch him. He's mine - mine." The young girl was flustered and for the first time a real fear was showing on her face. It could have been a mother's natural instinct to protect her child, or it could have been something else.

"But you must let us look at him. He may be ill or perhaps hungry." Petrov persisted.

The young girl was now plainly terrified and continued to resist the policeman's request and his attempt to get a look at the baby in her arms. "Not ill - not ill," she muttered.

"Come, let me look," Petrov said more firmly and he made

a tug at the shawl.

"No! No! Don't touch my baby!" The girl screeched and tried to stand up but the strong arm of the policeman forced her back onto the seat.

"You must let me look at the baby. It is not well. You know it is not well." He spoke sharply and to emphasise his impatience he took the girl's face in one large hand and twisted it to face him. "You know your baby is not well. I must look at it. You know that, don't you?"

The young girl tried to shake her head free from the policeman's grip and at length managed to do so.

Petrov turned back to the baby. "Come! Unwrap the child," he ordered sternly, "or it'll be the worse for you." To show that he meant business he took hold of the shawl and began to pull it away from the child.

The young girl was frantic. "No! No!" she shouted and fiercely fought to retain the baby, but the policeman was strong and had strong hands, which would not be denied.

Soon it was evident that a struggle was taking place for the possession of the infant. Though she could not hope to match the strength of the policeman, the young girl fought with a wild frenzy, which made his task difficult.

"No! No!" she continued to shriek. "Leave my baby! You shan't touch it!"

But her pleas were ineffectual.

As Petrov managed to unravel part of the shawl, so the girl quickly wrapped it back around the baby. But the policeman was determined.

The others watched anxiously and at one point Irina rose to intervene. She was pulled back by the small, shabby man who shook his head and motioned her to be quiet.

Irina did not understand his action. She felt that she must help the girl. "Why?" she whispered fiercely to the small man. "You must let me help her even if you will not." She was about to rise again when Petrushka whispered to her.

"Notice how strange it is that the baby has not woken." He was not smiling this time. His serious expression frightened

Irina who now began to understand.

"I must look at that baby. It is not well. In fact I believe it to be very ill, Comrade Mother." Petrov was relentless.

"Please. Leave me alone. Leave my baby alone." The young girl's tone had changed to a whimper but whatever method she used she could not shake off the policeman.

"I want to look at that baby. There is something wrong here and I mean to find out what it is. You may as well stop struggling for I shall find out. I always do." Petrov's face was hard and unrelenting, and his voice matched his looks.

To the others it was an unnerving spectacle but they somehow felt that they should not interfere but let the tussle continue. It was important to all of them.

Then Olga began to mutter something, barely audible and hardly intelligible. "It's gone. I know it. All gone. Dead – it's dead and gone. That's what he wants to know." She spoke to herself and did not address the others, but some of her words struck chill into the hearts of Irina and the student. As for Petrushka, he already knew.

"No! No! Please!" The young girl had become desperate and the contest for possession of the shawl or the child was growing wilder and more unmanageable. It seemed that it might go on for some time for as the policeman Petrov struggled to get hold of or a look at the baby, the young girl managed to get to her feet. The edge of the shawl was firmly in Petrov's s hands and as she stood to get away from him, the baby was suddenly pulled from her arms.

The young girl screamed as it tumbled to the floor with a sickening thud.

For a moment no one could do anything except stare in horror. Even Petrov was taken by surprise.

At that moment a blast from somewhere in the distance heralded the arrival of the train at the station of Kalinin. It was now a few minutes past four 'o clock, and there was no mistaking the fact that dawn was imminent.

Chapter Twelve
Kalinin

As expected the night train from Leningrad was right on time as it glided into the large empty station at Kalinin. For most of the passengers, who had been sensible enough to spend the hours since leaving Leningrad in getting some sleep, Kalinin would have meant nothing more than a few bright lights and a strange, echoing voice from the station loudspeaker. At that time of night, or rather morning, for it was almost four-thirty, any passenger who had chanced to wake from their sleep would have been lulled into thinking that it was still some sort of dream. There was an ethereal quality about that disembodied voice echoing through a deserted station, with all lights blazing but not a person in sight. Whether anyone had got on or off the train was difficult to tell. The voice continued to drone out its messages and directions, oblivious to the fact that for the Moscow express, the passengers therein were not one bit interested.

For those in the last compartment of the last carriage, arrival at Kalinin meant nothing more than that the train had stopped. Their attention at that time was wholly taken up with the events, which had so dramatically unfolded but a few minutes before the train had come to a halt.

All eyes were fixed on the bundle on the floor, the bundle, which had been wrenched from the arms of the young girl who, like the others, was now staring wide-eyed with a hand pressed across her mouth to stifle a further scream. No one had moved, though the student had made an involuntary gesture to catch the falling bundle - without success. Petrov the policeman was on his feet, and then one by one the others stood and closed around in a circle. Nobody spoke and the only sound heard in that compartment was the sharp, strained breathing of the young girl, like sobs with noise. As the others had edged in closer she remained completely still, and just stared with an unwavering steadiness at the object on the floor.

"Is…is it dead?" Olga whispered in an awe-struck voice. Despite her toughness and bleak opinion of the world, she had never actually seen a dead person before, not even a baby. Now the prospect was a mixed one of curiosity and dread at what would be revealed.

Petrov the policeman was about to bend down and examine the bundle when he straightened again. He motioned to the small, shabby man.

"You have a look. I don't trust my back to you lot."

Petrushka moved forward, knelt down and slowly and gently began to peel back the thick coarse shawl and other heavier wrappings. No one spoke and all eyes were fastened on the macabre unveiling.

As he unwrapped the body he carefully felt the form and shape perhaps to detect any broken limbs. He quickened the operation and to the consternation and surprise of the watchers he began to take less care as he feverishly scrabbled at the coverings. With a sudden final heave he had uncovered the child.

But it was not a child.

It was a doll, a large doll with a crack across its face caused during the tumble. The crack had split across one eye and made it look as though it was grinning at them.

The sight of the grinning doll brought a gasp or two from the watchers and was only slightly less horrifying than the smashed face of a child.

Petrushka picked up the mutilated doll no less reverently

than it had been a child and handed it to the cowering girl. Her eyes were full of terror and pain. She could not understand the gesture but she took the doll and held it to her, cradling it as if it had been a real child.

The others resumed their seats with the exception of Petrov, who knelt down and began to examine the shawl and other coverings.

"What do you expect to find, Comrade Policeman? Blood?" Petrushka did not attempt to conceal the sarcasm or contempt he felt for this man. "A doll, comrade. Is that your murder?"

Petrov was silent and ignored the remarks or appeared to. He turned to the girl. He had one of the coverings in his hand and he held it up to her. He was about to say something when suddenly the door was slid back and there was the conductress standing in the dull light from the corridor behind her like some apparition, or a wicked fairy godmother, come to take the child to her castle. Her voice dispelled the illusion.

"What was that screaming? What's going on here? I warned you, comrade," she said looking at Petrov, "that this is my train and you have no jurisdiction here. I want no trouble from any of you."

"And you'll get none if you mind your own business," Petrov growled at her.

She didn't seem to be overawed by his manner and just glowered back at him. "I know about you. You inspectors think you can get away with anything. Not in my train you don't. There's a load of tourists in the next compartment. A nice impression of our country they will take back to the West."

"Shut your mouth woman or I'll shut it for you." Petrov growled again without raising his voice or sounding angry.

The conductress was about to speak when he held a badge and a paper in front of her. It had the effect of stopping her in her tracks. Whether she had already suspected him of being a secret policeman or not, there was certainly something in what she saw which convinced her that this man Petrov was to be left alone. The colour drained from her cheeks and she began to move away.

"That is my first authority," he said, "and this is my other authority." Slowly he withdrew his revolver from his pocket and held it under her nose. It was enough, for she muttered something and swiftly disappeared sliding the door closed behind her. As she did so Petrov grabbed the young girl and pushed her back onto her seat, after putting the gun back in his pocket. He still had the piece of blanket in his hand, and the gun in the other. He now stood with his back against the sliding door and looked around at the others. He held out the piece of blanket for them to look at.

"Yes, comrades. There is blood on this piece of rag. But dolls do not bleed, as our learned friend was quick to point out. Well? What about it?" He thrust the blanket at the young girl who just twisted her head away, "I said murder - and nothing has happened to make me change my mind in that respect."

"You are still far from the truth of it, Comrade Policeman. So what? It does not signify that any crime has taken place. And are you sure that it is blood?" The small, shabby man was still prepared to cross swords with the policeman even though he did not know the truth of it himself. But he was willing to keep fighting for the sake of the young girl until Petrov made him shut up. He knew that sooner or later this brutal policeman would lose patience and want to keep him quiet on a more permanent basis. He was prepared to risk that.

The policeman, however, ignored Petrushka and held the piece of blanket in front of the girl's face.

"Well? Is it blood? Is it?"

Natalia didn't look at the blanket or the policeman. She just stared ahead with round unblinking *eyes*.

"Well? Answer me!" Petrov shouted. The policeman was growing impatient. He didn't like this kind of suspect, one who was remote and detached. He had met them before. Usually they said nothing at all under any kind of persuasion, or they were too pliable, too susceptible to any suggestion. It was no good to him if she just agreed to everything and it was no good if she wouldn't admit anything. He had to know her version of the truth. He could always twist it around to serve his own purpose later. "Tell me," he repeated more softly, "if is it blood?" He sat down beside her. "You may as well tell me the whole truth now. What have you done with your baby?"

The girl still did not move but she blinked several times like someone waking from a sleep.

The voice from the loudspeaker in the station was still issuing instructions in that ghost-like way, which echoed around the empty platforms. Though the echoing voice had an unreal quality about it, the passengers in that last compartment were reminded that they were still connected to the real world and that it was the events within which belonged to the nightmare.

No one could tell how long the train had stood waiting in Kalinin Station, perhaps only a matter of minutes but to them it was timeless. Only the final destination was important now and that was still some way off. The lights shone brightly on the empty platforms, which later in the day would be crowded with travellers all waiting to be taken to the capital city by the local train. The night train from Leningrad meanwhile was pausing to get its breath back before the final stretch of its journey. Outside the station, dawn was beginning to glimmer as the darkness was tinged with greyness at the edges. The night was still obscured by the station lamps, however, which shone cold and alien.

Inside the last compartment the young girl Natalia began to talk. She spoke so quietly that it was almost a whisper.

"My baby is dead," she said calmly, without emotion. She let the doll slip to the floor with a clatter.

"What about Boris?" The baby's father?" Petrov asked.

The girl looked puzzled and gave the policeman a strange smile. "No. The baby is not called Boris. The baby is dead, not Boris."

The policeman's sudden change in question had confused her and she

faltered. She screwed up her face trying to recall the events of the past. "My baby died. I didn't want him to die. I wanted

Boris to die," she said with a sudden outburst. "And I wanted to die too," she added quietly.

"That can be arranged," Petrov hissed with impatience. "Now tell me. Who is dead?"

"The baby is dead," the girl repeated. "I have told you."

"So you did. Did you kill it?"

The young girl said nothing for a moment while the others waited anxiously to learn whether she would deny this charge. It was as important for them as for the girl, for in some way they were all part of that accusation.

"I...I must have done. It was alive and now it is dead." The admission did not release any fear or remorse she may have felt and she settled back into her familiar silent stare.

Petrov turned round to the others with a grim smile of pleasure on his face. "Well. There we have it, the ultimate crime - infanticide. You see I was right. Everyone has something to hide; everyone has a secret; and everyone commits crimes." He laughed aloud. It was not a natural laugh, not a laugh of genuine amusement, but a terrifying, throaty gurgle of exultation. It was the laugh of one who had triumphed. Petrov the policeman had played out his game and won.

"So it is over now, is it?" The small, shabby man spoke up again. "May we be spared your gloating?"

"What's the point of being proved right if I can't enjoy my success?" He laughed again, exposing his large uneven teeth, like some prehistoric creature, which had just feasted upon a comrade. The only thing missing was the blood upon his fangs.

"What happens to her?" Irina indicated the girl as she spoke.

Petrov didn't seem bothered with her anymore. He glanced casually at the young girl and shrugged his shoulders.

"She'll be handed over to the authorities for further questioning along with the rest of you."

The passengers looked at each other with some anxiety as they realised that their ordeal was to continue beyond the journey.

"So it's not a game you were playing after all?" Irina spoke again.

"Game - game I Of course it was a game," Petrov exploded into another burst of animal laughter and then he paused and looked around at them. "But comrades, my games are always for real."

His words set a chill on the compartment. The lights in the station suddenly went out and the blackness once more surrounded them.

"You will all receive your just rewards for your crimes and, if you are lucky and very co-operative, I may let you off lightly." A flicker of a smile brushed his lips but no more than that.

"You!" Mikhail the student suddenly spoke up. "Will you interrogate us further? Haven't you done enough already, especially to that girl?"

Petrov showed no surprise or anger at this outburst. "Tut-tut, my young friend. Why should you worry about her, or any girl? I know where your real interests lie. But I will answer your question. Yes, I shall make certain that I will be the one to question you further. It can easily be arranged."

There was a further exchange of looks between them but no one was prepared to take issue with the secret policeman Petrov. They appeared to be resigned to the fact that he had won and had defeated them totally. He would devour them at his leisure.

"What about your evidence?" the small, shabby man said pointing at the doll on the floor.

Petrov looked down at the doll where it had fallen, at the feet of the student. He leaned forward to pick it up then hesitated as at the same time the student reached for it.

"Don't touch the evidence, Comrade Student. It will be needed."

He completed the movement but as he began to straighten up, with the doll in his hand, he felt something cold and hard pressed against the side of his head. He didn't have to guess at what it was. He knew the feel of a gun.

"Don't move, Comrade Policeman. Stay on your knees like the dog you are." The voice was that of the small, shabby man, but the gun, a small silvery thing, was firmly held in the cool, steady hand of the attractive Irina.

Petrov did not move. He had put too many other people in such a position to know what happens when someone tries to be clever. Invariably it ends with that person being shot.

"Take his gun," Irina whispered sharply and the student searched in the policeman's pockets until he had found it.

"Check for other weapons," the small man spoke again. "I'm sure he had another gun, or a knife or something."

Again the student searched through his pockets but it was not easy for him to check anything except the large coat, not while Petrov was in his kneeling position.

"Stand up!" Irina ordered with an added authority in her voice. "Now search him thoroughly," she commanded as the policeman slowly got to his feet, with the doll still in his hands and the gun still directed at his head.

The student could now make a thorough job of his search and he went through the policeman's pockets retrieving the items taken from them earlier, the bundle of roubles from Olga; the list of names from Irina and the packets of drugs from himself.

"Nothing, only these." He handed them to the girl and then stepped back to face Petrov.

"Sit down," Irina ordered the policeman.

Olga and the girl Natalia had meanwhile moved to the opposite seats so that now Petrov was face to face with all five other passengers.

"Not a very good policeman after all, are we, Comrade Vladimir Petrov. Before you begin to accuse people of crimes it's always best to make sure that they have no weapons - in case they should resent your questions." Irina spoke coldly and with a new sense of hardness in her voice.

During this sudden and dramatic turn around of power, Petrov had been more surprised and shocked by what had happened, but not afraid. At last he found his tongue. "So what do you expect to achieve by all this? You have only added to your crimes. If you stop this foolishness now perhaps I may be able to forget." He made as if to move.

"Don't move a muscle, Comrade Petrov," said Irina. "If you think that a woman of the street doesn't know how to use a gun and shoot straight, you'd better think again."

When Petrov saw from the look on her face that she meant what she said, he frowned. He would have to try a new tactic. "But you others, you will all be in trouble unless you stop this foolishness right now. Tell her!"

"It's no use appealing to us, comrade," the small, shabby man said. "You see. This is a conspiracy. We are all in it together."

For a moment Petrov thought he was going mad, or that his ears had deceived him. "But… but," he stuttered. "People just don't join together like that. You hardly know each other. It doesn't make sense."

"It makes perfect sense, Comrade Policeman." The young girl spoke up. She was no longer wide-eyed and staring but calm and self-assured. "We live in a state which was founded on co-operation by people like us. On our own we could not hope to overcome you, but together we are strong."

"And what makes you think that we don't know each other?" Olga piped up and smiled. "You see we do know each other, because we have each suffered. We know what it is like to suffer and that makes us one family, so to speak."

"You are so quick to judge, Comrade Policeman. You are so sure of the silence of your victims. You are so sure of their guilt. What about your own guilt?" Mikhail, the student, had lost all of his previous inhibitions and punctuated each of his remarks by jabbing the policeman's gun at Petrov.

Petrov, however, was not impressed with their words. He grunted and leaned back against the seat and sulked like a schoolboy. "You are fools," he muttered. "Soon we will be in Moscow and what do you think will happen then?"

"What do you think will happen comrade?" Petrushka said quietly, almost kindly, but his words had the distinct ring of menace.

For the first time Petrov experienced some unease and he began to wonder.

Petrushka continued. "You see, comrade, or rather you don't see, but you will, that all this," he waved his arm around the compartment and indicated his fellow passengers, "is designed specially for you. While you thought that you were playing games with us, in reality we were playing games with you." He paused to allow what he had said to sink in.

The policeman didn't seem moved and just glowered at him.

"You want to know what it is all about I suppose. I suspect you think that it is a game, which we have just made up on the spur of the moment. But consider, how could we? You have been here all the time and we have barely spoken to each other. That's one fact. The other fact is evident enough. We all seem to be part of some conspiracy against you. So don't you want to know how and why?"

Petrov was still not impressed. "You can talk till you're blue in the face but it doesn't alter the essential fact that you're all criminals and now you are in some sort of conspiracy to… to…"

"To do what, comrade? To murder you?" Petrushka spoke quietly and with an almost exaggerated politeness. "You don't think much of us if that is the case. Do you really think that we just happened to make all this up without any thought or planning? That we suddenly decided when you went to pick up the doll? That Comrade Irina should just happen to have a gun? Very coincidental don't you think?" Petrushka sat back and contemplated Petrov with raised eyebrows, inviting further comment.

Petrov wasn't going to let such an opportunity pass without saying something. "Are you trying to tell me comrade that all this is some sort of elaborate plot, arranged for my benefit?"

Petrushka nodded.

"Well I don't believe it," Petrov rasped. "You were my prisoner. I chose this compartment. You couldn't know anymore than I did. And how could anybody know that I would play my games?" He leered at Petrushka defying him to disprove what he had just said.

Petrushka merely smiled. "But comrade, you always play your games. You are well known for it. I might almost say famous for your humour. As for me being your prisoner, well, it was not too difficult to allow myself to be taken by you. I knew that we would go back to Moscow on the night train, provided I did nothing to get you mad enough to kill me. I was careful enough to give you no opportunity. You see, comrade, we know about your little idiosyncrasies, your peculiarities shall we say. It was an easy matter to let you believe that you were in charge."

Petrov listened to the words of the small man with a growing sense of disbelief. He had never been in such a situation before and kept on thinking that he was imagining everything. But the small silver gun, held by the steely-eyed Irina, was not part of his imagination, nor was his own, much heavier weapon, now in the hands of the student Mikhail. He tried to reason it out, to bring some logic and order into the situation. None of it made sense. He chuckled and then clapped his hands.

"Very good - very good. I admit that you have got your own back, comrades. However you did it doesn't concern me. I acknowledge defeat. I have been beaten at my own game." He chuckled again to emphasise his willingness to accept such an explanation.

His cheerfulness was met only by the stony stares of his fellow passengers. He looked at each one in turn hoping to find someone who would agree with his version and break down and confess it. There was no reaction. He licked his lips nervously. It was the first outward sign that he had shown to betray his unease and growing anxiety. He laughed again, still trying to encourage some response. There was still no reaction.

At length Irina spoke. "You never play games, comrade. That much we know about you. Your games are always for real. We have seen that for ourselves."

"But... but what's all this for? What do you hope to gain by keeping me here like this? We shall be in Moscow in three hours or less and then what?" He looked at them and narrowed his eyes. "You will have to kill me then, because I know you all and your crimes."

"We will talk about our crimes later. First, Comrade Petrov we shall look into your crimes," Irina replied coldly.

Petrov shook his head in perplexity. He couldn't really understand yet what was going on. He had never in the whole of his career been in such a position where a gun was being pointed at him and not at one of his luckless victims. And there was talk about his crimes. "What crimes? I have committed no crimes. I am a loyal servant of the state. Everything I do is for the security and welfare of the state. You have no right to set yourselves up as my judges."

"Right doesn't come into it comrade," Petrushka said pleasantly, "but for the moment we certainly have the power."

Petrov scowled at his former prisoner and began to understand what this was all about.

"Uh-huh. Revenge. Is that it? No fine ideals. Just plain, ordinary revenge for the tricks I played on you." He snorted with contempt but still no one was moved to challenge his assumption. This lack of response was becoming unnerving. It was like challenging ghosts to a duel. He didn't like it, and worse was that he didn't know what to do to reverse the situation and regain his former mastery. For now all he could do was to wait and go along with the charade or game, or whatever it was. It would have to finish before Moscow. That thought didn't entirely make him feel comfortable, however.

The last compartment of the last carriage of the night train from Leningrad had become a tiny theatre in which a drama had been slowly unfolding during the journey between the two capitals of Russia. At the moment the train was silently standing in the station at the small town of Kalinin, some two hundred kilometres from the present capital, Moscow. A third of the journey remained and outside, beyond the station and beyond the unreal glare of the lights, which illuminated nothing but empty platforms, the dawn was slowly creeping in. The cloak of darkness would soon be stripped back and the players in that last compartment would once more become part of the real world outside. But dawn was not yet arrived and they still had an hour or so in which to play their drama against the backcloth of the night.

Rather than showing any sign of fear, Petrov the policeman, was becoming bad-tempered. He had sunk back into the padded seat and thrust his hands into the deep pockets of his overcoat. He glowered at those who now held him prisoner and was determined to be as uncooperative as possible. The small gun was still aimed at him but it was not going to put him off. Barring accidents he had already reasoned that there was nothing they could do in the time. Soon the train would leave the station and then there would be no more than a couple of hours before it was light and the corridor outside would be busy with people and the conductress. The conductress! He had forgotten about her. She had to come in sooner or later if only to remind them of their arrival time. Then he had another thought. Would she really bother with this compartment? Had he not already made it abundantly clear that he wanted no interruptions? He cursed inwardly but how was he to know that such a situation would arise. He could only wait and find out if she kept to his instructions. These petty officials though, often felt that what they saw as their duty was more important than matters of state. He was confident, however, that she wouldn't be able to resist poking her nose into the compartment. He relied on it. But why wasn't the train moving? They had been here long enough. And why didn't these people get on with their game? They had held him for some time now. Were they just going to sit staring and pointing that silly, little gun at him? He expected something better than that. The idea, however, suddenly gave him a fresh surge of confidence. They are after all amateurs. No doubt of it. All he had to do was to keep his head and say what they wanted to hear then there would be no problem, not for him that is. But he would make very sure that there were plenty of problems for this lot. He would teach them to play games with him, Vladimir Petrov, secret policeman. They would know better next time, if there were a next time for any of them. If he had his way he would send them all off to some labour camp, if they were fit enough to travel after he had finished with them. He was struck by the humour of it. He had a strange sense of humour this Vladimir Petrov, secret policeman. He didn't yet realise it but he was going to need this sense of humour and more, much more.

The door of the compartment being slid back with a harsh grating sound rudely shattered Petrov's musings. He looked at the doorway and was both surprised and pleased to see the stocky figure of the conductress about to enter. He went to make a signal but stopped when he noticed that she expressed no surprise or shock at what she found in the compartment. It was though he was not there for she looked only at Irina, the one with the small, silver gun.

"We are leaving Kalinin in a few minutes, comrade. We shall arrive in Moscow at seven."

Irina smiled in acknowledgement and consulted her wristwatch. "We shall be ready," she murmured.

Before Petrov could say anything the sliding door clanged shut and the conductress was gone. He couldn't believe it. Hadn't she seen anything? Was she blind? Stupid? Or both? Then another thought occurred to him. Perhaps she too was part of this conspiracy. Perhaps it was she who had arranged for this carriage. Yet why had she been so uncooperative earlier on? She had behaved like any other conductress, jealous and proud of her title and precious train. He shook his head in some slight perplexity. She must have seen what was happening. It was almost as if he wasn't there and that no one was threatening him a gun. She must be part of it, he decided. That was the only explanation.

"We shall be moving soon, Comrade Policeman," Petrushka said, breaking into Petrov's thoughts.

"You must be mad, all of you. You can't hope to get away with it." Petrov affected an air of incredulity hoping to get one of them to explain all of this.

"Get away with what, Comrade Policeman?" Petrushka smiled mischievously. "You seem to be concerned with our fate. That is good of you, specially when it is your fate that is to be decided here, not ours."

Somewhere in the distance there was a snorted klaxon. Then silently the lights of the station began to move backwards. The night train from Leningrad was beginning the last stage of its journey. Soon the grey, deserted platforms had receded into the darkness of the night, which had suddenly clamped around the train as it gathered speed. It was now racing towards Moscow and the dawn.

Had Olga, the square faced woman, cared to peer out of her favourite window, she might have seen the edges of that blackness beginning to turn grey. But nobody was interested in looking out of the window. The passengers in that last compartment were much more interested in playing out their final scene.

"To while away the time until we reach our destination, we are now going to play a game," Irina suddenly said with a mocking ring in her voice, as she threw back Petrov's own words he had uttered earlier. "It is a two part game. The first part will prove how badly you played your game, not because you are now in our hands, but because you played by your own rules and made a total mess of your performance." She paused as she deliberated on the next words. "The second part of our game will not really be a game at all because we are not playing to your rules. The second part is more difficult for all of us as we have to decide how best to dispose of you."

The train had now reached its maximum speed but only a light rocking and a gentle, rapid click-click of the wheels upon the rails denoted this. To all of them in the last compartment of the last carriage it meant nothing.

For the first time since he had been threatened Petrov felt the icy trickle of fear creep down his spine.

"You mean…" He tried to hide the stammer in his voice by wiping his hand across his mouth. But it showed nevertheless.

"Yes. We are going to kill you," said Irina, without emotion.

Chapter Thirteen
Trial And Judgement

"As I said, the first part of our game is to show you how poorly you played your game." Irina turned to Olga. "You began with Olga here. It's not her real name of course, but as it happens she is exactly what she looks like, an average Russian housewife. She's no criminal."

"That bundle of roubles says different," Petrov said sulkily.

"Show him." Irina motioned to the student who passed the bundle to Petrov. "Look at them closely. Only the first half dozen or so are genuine. The rest are forgeries. Not brilliant forgeries but good enough to fool you. In fact they were specially prepared for you. Have a close look comrade, a real close look."

As she spoke Petrov began to flick through the bundle and as he did so he realised that upon closer examination that the notes were indeed very poor forgeries. He was puzzled. How could he have been so easily deceived? It didn't make sense. Fraud was not one of his specialities but he knew enough about forgeries to be able to spot one, even in the poor light of this carriage. He flicked through them again, pausing occasionally to check an individual note. They were not even proper forgeries. Some of them were blank on one side and the colours and printing were all wrong. They wouldn't have fooled anyone not even foreigners.

"They were good enough to fool you, comrade," Olga said and her square face became criss-crossed with a smile as she nodded at him like a child pleased with its own cleverness.

"So much for the roubles." Irina nodded to the student who took the bundle of useless paper from the policeman. "Now what about Mikhail here, the student?"

"I'm not a student really, not anymore. I have a job in Moscow, in a bookstore. I was in Leningrad visiting my parents." Mikhail handed the two small packets to Petrov, the very two that the policeman had confiscated earlier. "Open them and see what's inside."

The policeman took the packets almost reluctantly. He had an uneasy feeling that he was about to be confounded once again. Slowly he opened them and peered inside. There was nothing. They were empty, and yet when he had first been handed them he knew they contained substances like powder. He had felt the bulge of the packets. He could not have been deceived this time. Could he no longer trust his own eyes? Something strange was going on and he was determined to find out more. But how could it be? His puzzlement was obvious enough to make the student laugh out loud.

"Not very thorough are we, comrade?"

Petrov could bear being wrong or misled but he could not tolerate the smiling face of the student Mikhail, full of mockery. He wanted to do something violent to him. He lurched towards the young man but was halted by the stern reminder of his vulnerable position in the shape of his own revolver being pointed at him by the student. He sank back into the seat deflated but not completely dejected. His eyes continued to smoulder with a hatred, which kept pace with a sense of unease. The two emotions were finely balanced.

At a signal from Irina, the student took the packets from Petrov, who surrendered them without argument.

"Now let us turn to Natalia and see what a mess you made of that interrogation." Irina looked towards the young girl. "Tell him all about yourself Natalia."

The round staring eyes of the young girl, Natalia, were no

longer in evidence as she stood up and smiled brightly at Petrov.

"My name is not Natalia. We are all using different names. I live in Moscow like Mikhail here, and my parents are in Leningrad. As it happens I am married. My husband's name is Ivan. That is real. And we have a lovely baby daughter. This can easily be verified. I am hiding nothing." She spoke like a young girl giving her party piece on prize day. She spoke boldly and with total self-assurance, something, which had been lacking in that young girl with the baby. "You assumed I was guilty of a crime without a shred of evidence to support your belief. So I choose to cradle a doll like a baby. What of it? Perhaps I like dolls. Many grown-ups do you know. But you had already decided my crime, hadn't you. It was just a question of fitting what you saw into what best would make your theory work." She paused for a moment as a thought struck her. "Here. Look at that." She fished out from a pocket in her coat a photograph of a family group and handed it to Petrov.

The policeman studied the photograph carefully. He could certainly recognise the girl in it as the smiling wife and mother, with a young child clinging to her arm. The man must be her husband. Had he been fooled again or had he fooled himself? It was true that he had maybe taken too much for granted. She was right when he considered his earlier actions. He had to agree that he had nothing to go on except his instinct. Yet his instinct had never let him down before. It was also becoming increasingly apparent that this entire charade had indeed been arranged beforehand to lead him into thinking and believing certain things they wanted him to think and believe. When he thought back to the interrogation of the girl he realised that there had been no concrete evidence, not like the others, but her face and wide-eyed manner had made him think that there was something wrong. He had seen such looks before and always behind that kind of face there lurked the knowledge of murder. As he handed the photograph back to the girl he looked closely at her. There was no escaping the fact that she had radically changed. Instead of that wide-eyed stare and hollow face, her eyes shone bright and clear and her face seemed to have filled out. She looked like what she said she was, a young, happy, healthy wife and mother. As she took the photograph from him he detected the mockery in her eyes and knew that he had been fooled again. He wasn't sure whether he preferred to be fooled like this and suffer the indignity of their sneers, or to take whatever revenge they had in mind for him.

"And what about you?" Petrov said wearily to Irina. "You have left yourself till last, or are you going to forego the pleasure of exposing my apparent complete and total incompetence? It really doesn't matter. I suppose you have some splendidly contrived explanation." He allowed a small sigh to escape his lips. It was the first chink in the armour of this huge, forbidding policeman. Was he beginning to crack?

The thought that at last Petrov was beginning to understand the reality and the unreality of his situation must have pleased the rest of them. If so, it didn't register in their looks, which were oddly placid and affable. Irina was not quite ready to talk, not until she had laid down her small, silver gun beside her and reached into her small handbag, which lay with her case under the seat. She was taking no chances with Petrov although the student who was still closely watching him. Even as Irina moved, he took a step towards Petrov and held the heavy, black pistol against the policeman's temple. At length Irina had found what she was looking for and held it up for Petrov to see. It was some sort of card but it was closed and Petrov couldn't see any details.

"I have left myself till last, Comrade Petrov because I think I will surprise you the most. Show him the list Mikhail."

Without taking his eyes or the gun off Petrov, the student fumbled   in his pocket for the piece of paper on which earlier Irina had scribbled some names and addresses. He handed it to the policeman.

"Look at the names closely comrade," Irina said quietly, "and the addresses."

Petrov took the paper and looked at it. The list of names was still there. What was she on about he wondered? Then suddenly it hit him. Why hadn't he noticed before? These names. It was too silly for words. How could he not have noticed? The light wasn't that bad for him not to have made out names like 'Leo Tolstoy' or 'Fedor Dostoevsky', and certainly he would have noticed 'Vladimir Ulyanov.' There was something very wrong here. He looked at the addresses. 'The Winter Palace', 'The Kremlin' - it didn't make sense. As the words swam before his eyes mocking him far more than the smiles from the conspirators, he began to wonder whether he wasn't experiencing some extraordinary life-like dream. Perhaps he would wake up and everything would be in its proper place again. Or maybe he was going mad. Nothing was certain anymore. It was all confusion. He didn't even notice when the piece of paper was taken from him.

"And now, Comrade Policeman, here is another piece of paper for you to read." Irina opened up the card in her hand and held it before Petrov's face. For the first time his eyes showed something like fear.

"You do well to be afraid. When you thought that you had a high-class whore to deal with, there was nothing to fear from such a person. But I am not what you supposed me to be unlike the others here, I do have some real power, and the sort of power which you will the more appreciate."

Petrov was looking at the small picture and the words on the card in front of him and he was not only further puzzled but perhaps for the first time he felt a very definite vulnerability. His unease was quickly becoming anxiety for he would never admit, even to himself, that he was afraid. Yet he knew that he should be afraid, for this attractive, fair haired woman, with the steely blue eyes, was no less a personage than a major in his very own secret service. That in itself explained much – the gun, the self assurance even when under interrogation. He knew there was something special about her from the beginning. This made everything different. He knew his own people. If they suddenly thought him to be expendable they would not hesitate to eliminate him. He licked his lips again at the thought and yet...

"Comrade Major I don't understand. Why should you...?" He found himself spluttering and out of his depth. To find a high party officer here with these others, who it seemed after all were only ordinary citizens, was too much to comprehend.

"There's much you don't understand, comrade and much you have to learn about police work," Irina said grimly. "Now that you aware of my true identity, you are perhaps more suitably impressed. You also know that I can and will use this." She picked up the small silver gun, having already slipped the card into her handbag, and pointed it at him. It did not give her any great satisfaction to see him flinch or to behold the furtive, frightened look in his eyes. In fact at that moment Irina felt nothing for this man. Even the mark on her face, where he had struck her, was faded, though later there would no doubt be some sort of bruise. "The first part of our game is practically over. We have shown how inefficient and incompetent you are as a policeman. In not one case did you do the proper things. You made no real enquiry into our backgrounds. You made no search of our possessions, except for her." She waved her gun in the direction of Olga. "You simply guessed or assumed because you wanted your own theories to be right. It was just a game and it didn't matter if the facts, such as they were, didn't quite fit. You were only interested in finding each one of us guilty." Irina paused and looked coldly at the big man before her. "How often have you used the same procedure, comrade? How often have you played these kinds of games? How many people have you condemned in this way?"

Petrov was listening but wasn't really concentrating upon what the attractive Irina was saying. He was still trying to come to terms with the situation. It was so odd because certain things kept haunting him but he didn't know why. It was as if everything had happened before and yet it was different. If only he could reason it out. He was sure that he must have overlooked something. There was a vague familiarity about all of these people but the sensation was too flimsy to grasp hold of. He couldn't think properly anymore, not with that gun pointing at him. He knew he was sweating. He couldn't help it, nor could he hide it. They must know that he was uneasy and afraid. Yet he wasn't sure of exactly what he was afraid. Death - perhaps, but he sensed it was something more than that. It was the whole thing. It was like he was on trial. That's it! He was on trial. "I'm on trial," he suddenly spluttered aloud

"So you have guessed comrade," the small man said. "Yes, you are on trial. We have already established your credentials and the witnesses have established theirs. How would it be then if I were to be the judge?" The small man beamed warmly and his smile was in odd contrast to the grim faces of his companions.

Petrov could understand the pleasure that Petrushka would get from playing such a part. It was only natural with him being a suspect criminal likely to receive a maximum penalty. The others seemed less concerned with pleasure. For them it looked like a matter of revenge. He could not think why. Even the games he had played on them surely did not warrant such treatment. Straightforward revenge - yes, but this drawn out facade of a trial was altogether too much. It was too ridiculous. Besides, he reasoned, there would be precious little time before they reached Moscow. Whatever it was they wanted, they would have to make up their minds quickly without all this fuss. Yet there had to be something more to this farce, especially as it involved an officer of the service. It must be something he had done or knew about. What it could be though completely baffled him. All he could do was to let them get on with it and look for a chance to turn the tables.

The swaying of the carriage and the ever-increasing click-click of the wheels upon the tracks gave Petrov some reassurance. The train was now at its maximum speed. There was only about two hours before they reached their destination. He would have to use all of his wits and play for time.

"Why don't you get on with whatever you have decided to do?" Petrov said in a surly, almost defiant manner. "We shall be in Moscow soon and then you will have to end your little game."

Irina looked across the carriage out of the window. She

knew he was right. Already the blackness, which had shrouded them since the start of the journey was becoming decidedly less opaque, and vague shadows of the changing countryside, began to fly past. They would have to move quickly.

"Comrade Vladimir Petrov you are indicted of crimes against the Russian people. For that you are to be judged."

Petrov just smiled. "That's absurd. What Russian people?"

Mikhail the student spoke. "Andrei Platov, a bookseller, an old man, my grandfather. You picked him up two years ago on suspicion of distributing banned literature. He died under torture, a torture which you took pleasure in administering. He was innocent but you didn't let that stop you."

"Mari Dubrotskia - widow with two small children - my sister." It was Olga's turn. "She was picked up a year ago on a charge of shoplifting. She was cleared but too late to prevent her death at the hands of the interrogating policeman in charge - Vladimir Petrov."

"Josef Kuratin, a young man just married, a laboratory assistant - my brother. Suspected, only suspected, of selling drugs and was picked up for questioning. There was no evidence but that didn't stop a certain policeman from questioning him. He died as a result of those questions. The policeman - Vladimir Petrov." Natalia the young girl added her own accusation.

Petrov listened to the catalogue of his crimes without showing any change of expression. "Is that all? What about you, Comrade Major? Surely you must have something to accuse me of?"

"Peter Brodski - doctor, dedicated to the service of others. He disappeared and was later found dead. The truth of his death would never have been discovered until I learned that he had threatened to expose a certain Vladimir Petrov to his superiors for the torture and death of suspects. Suspects who were all found to be innocent. The doctor discovered this practice when, working at the prison, he was called to revive a dying man. The doctor was my husband." Irina betrayed no emotion in presenting the final charge.

For a while there was an uneasy silence. The only sound was the rhythm of the train as it swallowed up the miles.

"You have heard the charge, Comrade Policeman. How do you plead?" Petrushka stared at Petrov, his eyes twinkling in mischievous anticipation.

Petrov just glowered at him.

"We want to do things properly, comrade," the small man said by way of explanation.

"You're enjoying this nonsense. You may as well because it won't be for long."

"Tut-tut," said Petrushka in mock disapproval. "You don't seem to realise what a delicate position you're in. These are serious charges. Do you have anything to say in answer to them?"

Petrov remained silent.

"You must say something, comrade. It is you right - before we pass sentence."

Petrov gave an ironic chuckle. "That's good of you, comrade. It is my right, is it - and before sentence is passed? Is there really any point in me saying anything? It's all decided. Never mind whether it's true or not."

"It is true," Petrushka said eagerly. "We should like you to confirm it. After all we have demonstrated to our mutual satisfaction that you do not really bother about evidence."

"How should I know? You mention names, which mean nothing to me. In each case it was some time ago, too long to remember from among all my cases. You could say anything, pick out any name and say I was responsible." Petrov narrowed his eyes and looked keenly at both Petrushka and Irina. "You could be making it all up, or you could be basing your accusations on insufficient evidence. You have accused me of such a thing. Why not yourselves? I see no evidence. After all isn't that the point you are trying to make?" Petrov felt pleased with himself. He had seen an opening - a flaw in their argument. If they were the instruments of justice, as they liked to think themselves, they would be the first to play by the rules. He knew it and so did they. What if all they said was true? How should he remember anyway? It had been a long time ago and there had been many names, many faces. It was part of the job. So a few people died - if they were innocent - hard luck. There must have been something about them to arouse suspicion in the first place. "In any case, comrades," he continued, "my duty was not concerned with innocence but guilt. Everybody is guilty of something. It was my place to discover the exact nature of that guilt. Besides, my superiors were always quite happy with my work. There were never any complaints." He smirked as he relaxed against the seat. "Do your worst. You cannot harm me."

Petrushka looked serious. "I see," he said slowly. "So your defence to these charges is that firstly there is no evidence against you, and secondly that anything you did was upon orders from your superiors. Is that how I am to understand it?"

Petrov nodded and smirked again. "If you like. You are bringing the charges. All I have to say is - prove it."

"Oh dear," said the small, shabby man with a resigned shake of his head. "You are right of course. We must prove our case. Not like the way that you prove yours, upon supposition and instinct."

Petrov ignored the barb and just grinned. The tide was turning. He knew people, even the worst kind of people, and invariably they all liked to play by some kind of rules, that is why he always won. He had no rules. People were such fools. They made it easy for him, just like this lot were doing now with their pretence of dispensing justice. What did they know about such things? He looked out of the window and noted with some satisfaction that dawn was gradually overtaking the night. There was only an hour or so to go. He could wait.

The five passengers who sat opposite Petrov did not show any dismay or sign that their case was not a strong one, and one by which their own rules of procedure they would have to relinquish. In fact if anything they looked more implacable than before. They did not heed the fast approaching dawn or concern themselves with the reducing miles and minutes. They just sat staring at the man in front of them, each with a cold hatred in their eyes.

Irina, the attractive one, the major in secret intelligence and now the chief prosecutor was the first to speak. "If it is only a matter of evidence comrade I think we have sufficient for our purpose."

Petrov just grunted.

"First," she continued, "there is myself. Since my position in the Service affords me the use of all sorts of files and records, I was able to obtain a variety of evidence. In fact comrade, it might interest you to know that when I searched through those records about my husband, I also discovered information regarding others who had been disposed of in the same way. The circumstances were too similar to ignore and I began to dig deeper. Without burdening you with all the details I found sufficient evidence to link you, Comrade Policeman with these crimes and many more. For my own purposes, however, I needed a few accomplices to carry out what I had intended to be some form of retribution. We would also be acting for all those others who have suffered a loss in the way we have. To lose someone is bad enough but to lose someone to the brutality of a man like you demands some sort of retribution. We have the evidence comrade, be assured of that."

"Where is it then? I don't see it. Words are not evidence, even the words of a senior official in Intelligence. You accused me of ignoring the facts. Now you are doing the same." Petrov was gloating for he knew that he was right. If that's all they could bring against him then there was nothing they could do to him. He knew how such proper minds worked.

"Again comrade you are right," said the small, shabby man, and with another resigned shake of his head. "Believe us, we have such hard documentary proof that links you with a vast number of crimes but unfortunately this is a small compartment. We were aware that there would be practical difficulties in presenting strong evidence."

"But it satisfies us!" Olga suddenly shouted, as she interrupted the flow of the small, shabby man. "We know you to be guilty and that's enough for us."

"Is it?" said Petrov calmly. "Are you so certain that your comrades agree with you?"

Olga glared at him, her square face belching hatred for this man who had earlier humiliated her.

"It's no good puffing yourself like a frog. That doesn't tell me anything except how ugly you are." Petrov was not afraid to sneer at her. "What about the rest of you?" He turned to the young woman and the student.

"I'm satisfied," Natalia said simply. "If ever I wanted confirmation of your guilt, your performance earlier convinced me that you were the kind of man who would do anything. I don't need more proof."

"I'm satisfied too." The student echoed the young girl's sentiments. He raised the policeman's pistol and pointed it at Petrov. "If it were left to me I would finish you now, comrade and be done with it."

A look of alarm crossed Petrov's face. Being right was one thing but who knows what headstrong youth may do. Perhaps he had misjudged them after all. He gave an inward sigh of relief when the student lowered the gun.

"But - we have agreed that it shall be done properly, so I will not shoot you yet." Mikhail lowered the pistol but still cradled it in his hands.

Petrov felt easier for he had not bargained for such hatred. Hatred was a sticky commodity for it often made people do things, which were not always in their own best interests. "And what about you, comrade?" He looked at Irina. He was sure of her, despite those cold, blue eyes. She would do things properly, of that he was certain. "Where is this evidence then?" He threw out the question as a challenge and dared her to answer it.

"We are satisfied," said the attractive Irina with a hard edge to her voice. "That is enough for us. Had you been in a courtroom you would have been overwhelmed with such evidence as you now crave to save your own skin. Yet you gave little regard to such evidence when it came to others. Here it is not practical nor do we have the time."

Her reference to time made them all aware that it was fast growing light. Now the dull greys and dirty whites of a vague inchoate landscape could be distinguished through the windows of the compartment. There were no details of the exact nature of the countryside through which they were passing, except for the occasional clump of tall dark pine. It would not be too long before there came signs of habitation.

"Knowing how eager and scrupulous you are about evidence, we have something else - a witness." Irina could not keep the sarcasm out of her voice.

Petrov frowned. How could that be? There were never any witnesses to his interrogations, only when confessions had been extracted. There had to be a witness to them. "A witness?" He looked at Irina and then at the others as if trying to make up his mind as to who it was likely to be, but he gained nothing from their faces. He looked again at Irina and studied her. He couldn't really believe that there had been any witnesses to anything he had done. In any case why should he worry? He only acted under orders.

"You look puzzled, Comrade Policeman," Petrushka said smoothly. "Look no further. I'm the witness."

Petrov's amused glance at the small man questioned the statement. How could it be, he was still asking himself?

Petrushka took no notice of the policeman's disbelief. "I witnessed many things when I was in prison but I will not bore you with the details of my experiences there. I will relate one incident only. It was two years ago, I think, when I had been picked up on a charge of vagrancy, with no visible means of support, but then how many of us do have visible means of support." He smiled at Petrov but allowed the smile to freeze on his face as he suddenly became serious. "Anyway, how or why I was there is not relevant. It is enough that I was in a cubicle awaiting interrogation when I heard sounds in a room next to me. It was the sound of voices, mostly one person's voice - your voice, Comrade Petrov. You have a very distinctive voice. The other voice was not nearly so definite but I could hear what was being said and the manner of its saying. The

John C Hayes

other person was an old man. I knew this because earlier I had seen him placed in that room, I heard you question him, much in the same way as you questioned my friends here a short time ago. It was your usual mixture of brutality and sly insinuation, and the usual threats against his family. Whatever it was that you wanted from him, he obviously was not going to give you. Even in the next cell I could tell that. At first I thought you were a fool for not seeing it, but then I listened to you run through the whole of your repertoire of persuasion and I realised that you were not interested in anything he had to say. In fact it seemed to me that you were glad he could tell you nothing for it gave you more time to question him. Was it like that with all your victims?" The small, shabby man looked at Petrov with an enquiring stare.

The policeman said nothing and looked casually out of the window to indicate his indifference.

"I was in my cell for hours and you were in the next one interrogating that old man for the same length of time. I heard thuds and bangs, and an occasional whimper of pain. I thought that I should go mad if I had to listen to much more of it. Not seeing what you were doing only made it worse. I have a good imagination you see. I heard one or two screams, sort of strangled, not piercing like a woman's, and then more questions. There were always more questions. I was beginning to wish the old man would make up something, confess to anything rather than have to endure your questions. At length it was finished and at the same time I was taken out of my cell. We almost collided, you and I comrade, as you came out of the adjoining cell. You were smiling and wiping your brow. He must have been a tough one I found out later that the old man's name was Andrei Platov - a bookseller by trade I believe." Petrushka paused. "You know the name, comrade?"

Petrov shook his head. "I've told you before. The name means nothing to me."

"Oh but it does, comrade. You were not listening. It was this young man's grandfather."

A flicker of interest crossed the policeman's face and for a moment he had visions of the gun in the student's hand being fired at him. He glanced wearily at the student but saw no sign that he was about to do anything. He was just sitting like the others, watching and listening, no emotions, neither sorrow nor hatred. Just sitting. It worried him when people didn't show emotions. He couldn't do anything with such people.

"I didn't quite finish my tale, comrade. The old man, who you now remember as I can see by your face, never came out of that cell alive. As I was being led back to my own cell I saw two warders carrying him out on a stretcher. His face was not covered though it should have been. You have much strength comrade and your hands are very large. I know what it is like to be struck by you, and so does Comrade Major."

"Have you anything to say before we pronounce sentence?" Irina picked up her small silver gun and held it loosely in her lap, like a symbol of her office as prosecutor.

"What sentence? What evidence?" Petrov was still not overawed by the situation and was not going to surrender without a fight. "A stupid old man as a witness. Some witness! He was only guessing. That is not evidence. And all your other so called evidence. It is not here. Well, it is here that counts. You say you cannot produce it. I say that you cannot pass sentence without solid evidence. I see nothing." He folded his arms and defied them to do their worst.

Petrushka looked at Irina and then at the others. For a moment they seemed to waver. They realised that this policeman was right. In the cold light of day, which was even now smearing the windows with dull, indistinct patterns, they wondered if they could proceed with the trial.

"We must decide," he whispered urgently to her, "and soon."

Irina, tight lipped, looked at Petrov, her eyes seeming to pierce him, and then turned to the others. "We know that what he is says is true," she said, "but we also know that we have the right of it. We cannot draw back now. We mustn't."

The others were reluctant to commit themselves and tended to avoid looking directly at Irina or Petrushka.

Mikhail the student voiced their feelings. "We were so sure when we set out from Leningrad. It was dark and what we had to do was best done in the dark. That's why we were told to take the night train. Since then much has happened and now it is almost light. Somehow it all looks different and even you agree that legally we have not presented a case against this man. We are not so sure now."

"We will abide by your decision," Olga said. She also had a nervous look and seemed not to want anything more to do with it. "Whatever decision you make it will be alright with us."

Irina looked at the eager, square faced Olga and could understand why she had suddenly got cold feet.

"What about you two?"

"It's like he said," Natalia nodded towards the student. "It seems different somehow to what we thought it would be, but I'm still prepared to stand by any decision you care to make."

"Me too." Mikhail nodded.

Irina turned to Petrushka and raised her eyebrows. "Do you feel the same?"

"When you have been in a cell with this man, and have seen what he can do, there is no way you would let him escape." For the first time the small, shabby man made no attempt to disguise the loathing he felt for the policeman. "It only needs for us to be agreed. If only one of us is against it, then we all are jeopardised. We must have total agreement because that is our strength."

"Well it seems that we have that I suppose," said Irina but she didn't sound very confident. She was resigned to a situation with which she herself was not entirely happy. She would like to have presented something stronger by way of evidence. It was necessary that this man Petrov knew that he was being sentenced in accordance with the correct procedure. Although she and the others were convinced of his guilt she still wanted him to acknowledge it. She wanted him to know that he was being given the opportunity that he never gave his victims. For all their sakes this thing had to be done properly. She was not too bothered about the policeman or what he may think.

Petrov began to chuckle quietly to himself. He could see what was happening. They wanted to get him their way, the correct way. But they couldn't and it made them feel guilty. Fools, he thought to himself. He wouldn't have gone through all that nonsense. If he had wanted to get rid of someone, a bullet in the head was the most efficient. It amused him to see these so called upholders of justice falter in their resolve.

"Why do you smile, Comrade Policeman? Do you not realise the perilous position you are in?" The small, shabby man, Petrushka, having thrown off his cloak of friendliness and good humour, now spat out his question with a surprising venom while his eyes blazed with a hatred which had suddenly turned him into a different man.

Though slightly perturbed by the change in attitude of this Petrushka, Petrov still smiled. "What pathetic avenging angels you do make. So now you are not sure what to do. That comes of trying to do things the right way. Expediency, comrades is the only answer when it comes to people, not conscience, not justice, not fair play or anything that may resemble it. Expediency has always been my watchword. In that way everybody is treated fairly. That's what you want to do, isn't it? You want to treat me fairly but you can't." He unfolded his arms and looked straight at Irina. "You may be an officer but how often have you put a gun to someone's head and squeezed the trigger. Eh? Not often, if at all I'll bet. Well, I have, dozens of times - because it was necessary. Hmm." He paused and grunted in satisfaction. "But you won't do it. I know your kind. None of you would do it. Whatever kind of distaste you may have for me, you still could not use the gun. And do you know why? Because you don't have the kind of guts it takes to… " He could have gone on with his taunts but there was something in the look that the attractive woman shot at him that made him think that it would be unwise to continue in this vein. Also he remembered the young student who had his own gun and might be provoked into using it against his better judgement.

"You are sure of yourself, comrade," Irina said, wishing that he had continued with his mockery, for she could feel her resentment and anger boiling up at the man's words and that sneering look on his face. It would have been much easier to kill him then, and she suspected that the others would feel the same. She was certain that they would only feel the more conscience stricken afterwards. It was better to come to a decision in cold blood.

Petrov just shrugged his shoulders but wouldn't say anymore.

"Well? Are we agreed then?" Petrushka asked impatiently.

Irina nodded.

Petrushka stood up and pointed to Petrov.

"You have heard the evidence against you. Though you choose to ignore it we do not. We have heard your defence. In our opinion it is no defence. Despite your scheming and clever twisting of words, you have long since convicted yourself by your own earlier actions. We therefore pronounce you guilty and the sentence is - death."

Petrov said nothing but just stared stonily in front of him. Outside it was getting lighter and in the early greyness, more distant images were now flashing past the windows of the carriage. Great tracts of flat areas, still snow covered, were broken by clumps of trees. There were no houses yet to be seen. There was at least another hour, maybe a little more, before the journey was complete. Whatever was to be accomplished must be done soon. They all knew this including Petrov himself.

It grew dark outside again as the train cut through great masses of tall pines interspersed with the equally prolific silver birch.

Once more silence had settled on the small group of passengers in the last compartment of the last carriage. It seemed that the silence was eternal. There were no more words to say. Both the accusers and the accused realised that words would no longer bring them back from the precipice, which they had now reached. Nothing could be said to alter the situation.

Perhaps it was that small group of passengers - the

conspirators - who were most affected by the way that events had progressed. They were not prepared for what they had always regarded as the inevitable. They knew in their hearts that it was not so much a matter of justice but of expediency, just as Petrov had said. If they were right to judge, were they also right in carrying out the sentence? Those thoughts were running through their minds even as the train was speeding through this stretch of woods. They would have to act quickly.

One of them, however, was totally convinced of their course of action.

"We must get rid of him now, while we are travelling through this stretch of countryside. I know this route and it won't be many miles before the first houses start showing up. We can't afford to waste the opportunity." Petrushka was almost pleading with Irina.

He had changed since the beginning of the journey. All his previous ironic humour was gone and no more did he smile at Petrov. He was more determined than the others to see that this brutal policeman be made to pay for his crimes. He had no finer feelings or qualms of conscience like the rest of them. He had seen what Petrov could do and the only way to deal with people like that was to get rid of them as quickly as possible. In that philosophy he was remarkably like Vladimir Petrov.

"We do not have your fervour, Comrade Petrushka," Irina said to the small, shabby man, "though I understand your motives. No doubt we all would feel as unequivocal as yourself had we undergone the same treatment as you have done, but you must allow us a little time to adjust to the idea of killing in cold blood."

"Then let me do it," Petrushka said excitedly. "Give me your gun and I'll finish the job now." He held out his hand to the student Mikhail, who at first didn't seem inclined to yield up the weapon he had taken from the policeman. As he began to change his mind Irina interrupted.

"No. I will carry it out. It is safer that way. I shall not be questioned, as any of you will be. No more. I will do it."

"Well, do it quickly then," the small, shabby man muttered.

Irina turned to Mikhail. "Check the corridor. See if it's clear."

As the young student was about to carry out this order, the sliding door was suddenly swished back with a clatter. It was the conductress.

"An hour to Moscow. You'd better be quick."

Without another word she disappeared. She had again ignored the presence of the two weapons. Before she could close the door Mikhail had slipped into the corridor.

A moment later he reappeared. "It is clear but we must be quick. The tourists further down the corridor are awake and soon they will be all over the place. You know what tourists are like."

"You go first and make sure that no-one comes up to this end." She indicated Natalia who joined Mikhail outside.

"Keep him covered. If he makes any movement, shoot him. Don't worry about me. If I'm careless enough to get in the way that's my bad luck,"

Mikhail nodded. Now they were finally going to do something he felt a lot better. It was all that talk that got him on edge. "You go down there and keep an eye on those tourists," he whispered to Natalia. As she glided past him, he took up a position at the door with the heavy, black revolver, belonging to the policeman, held in both hands and pointing into the compartment.

Petrov himself had listened to the final arguments and realised that despite any misgivings or finer feelings, they were going to carry out their intention of killing him. He had become increasingly alarmed at the way things had developed and though he had not given up hope that he might yet persuade the others of the illegality of their actions, he could not get around the blind hatred and thirst for vengeance of this shabby, little man, Petrushka, the clown. That was a grim joke in itself. The one from whom he thought that he had nothing to fear was the one who was least likely to be persuaded.

As he witnessed the preparations for departure from the compartment, for the first time he began to feel afraid. It was a sensation he could do without. He realised that at last they were going through with their plan. Even the conductress was in the plot with them. She must be because she had made no comment regarding the guns. He was indeed lost, unless there was some last minute change of heart. He could only hope now that they had left it too late and that they were too close to habitation to risk pushing a dead body onto the line.

Irina stood, as did Olga. She held the small, silver gun against Petrov's temple.

"Get up! If you don't I can just as easily put a bullet in your brain while you sit. And when you do stand, do it slowly. No sudden movement or he will put a bullet into your brain." She indicated Mikhail who was standing in the corridor with the pistol still pointing into the compartment.

Petrov slowly rose to his feet and as he did so Irina moved behind him.

"Walk to the door," she ordered and jabbed him with her gun.

Petrov began to move into the corridor, slowly and stiffly, like a man walking to the gallows.

Chapter Fourteen
Execution

Now that it was no longer dark, the sensation of speed became more apparent as the changing panorama flashed past the windows of the carriage. It was a sharp, cold day outside. Though mid April, the temperature was below zero and the ground was still covered in large patches of snow, the last dregs of winter. These would quickly disappear within the next week or so as the sun's warmth begins to creep into the land. The tall pines had stood as imperturbable sentinels during the icy blasts of the previous months and, bereft of needles, they presented a gaunt, sparse reminder of the harshness of the Russian climate. Their only companions were the unusually large number of silver birch sprinkled like tinsel among them. They somehow seemed out of place among the more durable pine, yet at the same time gave the impression that spring was not far away. They had survived the winter and now waited patiently for the life-giving rays of the sun to draw them into life. The Russian people were also patient and could also wait a little while longer.

These images of broken, snow-clad landscapes, however, did not intrude upon the group of people, who even now were manoeuvring into the corridor of that last carriage of the night train from Leningrad. If any of them had taken the trouble to look at what was passing by outside they would have seen only a vast, remote, desolate area without habitation, the ideal place for the dropping of a body where it could not be found for some time, if at all.

The big man Petrov was hustled and prodded towards the rear of the corridor, until he stood in the small space next to the conductress's cabin. As soon as she had caught a glimpse of the group moving along the corridor towards her, she had locked herself in her self-contained room among the dials, levers, computers and various bric-a-brac of her own quarters. She did not want to know what was taking place outside in the corridor.

It was too crowded for all six of them to squeeze into that small platform area at the end of the coach, so Natalia and Olga were despatched to keep intruders away. Already there were sounds emanating from the other compartments further down the corridor and the occasional tousled head poked out from a sliding door to be quickly withdrawn when it caught sight of the forbidding group clustered near the conductress's cabin. Soon people, mostly tourists, would be emerging and making their preparations to disembark. Already a few, random suitcases were being placed in the corridor in readiness for the luggage carts waiting at Moscow. It was always the same with tourists. They cluttered up everything and everywhere with their piles of luggage, expensive and fancy. They always refused to understand anything of the Russian language and were constantly asking questions and in general being a nuisance. The younger ones were not so bad. They seemed to be a lot better behaved. Perhaps it was because they were under the control of some responsible adults.

Irina and the others could only hope that this particular batch of tourists would behave and allow them to complete their task without any interference. It could be dangerous for them if they even suspected anything of what was going on.

She motioned the young student to stand behind Petrov as she tapped at the cabin door. After some muffled words the door slid open just an inch or two and the anxious face of the conductress appeared.

"I'm not coming out," she growled. "You'll have to do what you came for without my help. That was our agreement."

"We can manage," Irina muttered, "but we must have no interference from them." She pointed down the corridor. "Two of us will keep an eye on them but you have more authority and can always keep them in their compartments till we are finished."

The conductress wasn't happy, but the sight of the small silver gun in Irina's hand made her think that perhaps after all it would be better if she was around to prevent a rush of inquisitive tourists from getting in the way. She nodded.

"Be quick. I must make sure that they are all awake or we shall never have them ready to leave when we reach Moscow." Straightening her uniform and adjusting her cap she squeezed past Olga and Natalia and took up a patrolling position further along the corridor.

Irina turned to the others. "Let's not waste any more time. By the door, comrade." She nudged Petrov to the door of the carriage as the student and the small, shabby man took up their positions behind him.

Petrov, conscious of the two guns trained on him, gave a wry smile.

"So this is to be my execution platform eh? What will you do? Make me jump like a parachutist. I might survive. Then I would come back and hunt you all down. You know that. Don't you think that you're taking a chance?"

"Look out of the window, comrade." Irina tapped the window beside her. "See how the ground is travelling, so fast that it is no more than a blur. We are giving you a chance, Comrade Petrov. It is not much of a chance but a better one than you gave my husband or any of your other victims. They had no chance once they were in your hands. Be grateful for that chance, comrade, and take it."

"He doesn't deserve any chance," Petrushka growled. "And besides, what if he did survive? He would come for us alright."

"He's right, comrade."

Mikhail the student once more was allowing his

nervousness to get the better of him. Now they had reached the point of no return he began to sound unsure about the whole thing. "Could we not...?"

"No!" Irina snapped. "He must jump and take his chances. If he does survive it will only mean that we will have to hunt him down again. He knows that. You do know that, comrade, don't you?" She looked at Petrov who returned her stare but said nothing, "Open the door."

She prodded the policeman who, after a moment or two of struggling, managed to push open the heavy door, which swung backwards against the body of the carriage with a heavy thump.

The sudden rush of cold air almost took their breaths away and was strong enough to be felt down the other end of the corridor. The two women, Olga and Natalia, came running up.

"Is it over?" Natalia asked breathlessly but the excitement on her face soon disappeared when she saw the figure of the policeman standing by the open door.

"Push him out!" urged Olga, her voice shrieking with a feverish excitement and crackling in the cold. "Soon it will be too late." She cackled nervously and rubbed her hands together.

"I say we should kill him first," Petrushka hissed, "then we have nothing to worry about."

Irina thought for a moment. What the small, shabby man said made sense. At least it would be over quickly and completely with no looking back. Yet she couldn't just kill in cold blood like this. She may be in the service herself but it was no part of her job to be a murderer.

Petrov quickly noted Irina's indecision was, and seized his opportunity.

"Comrades. What is past is past. Whatever you think or imagine I have done is just not true. I can also bring evidence."

He had to shout the words in order to overcome the noise of the roaring wind rushing past the door, but the pleading in his tone was still unmistakeable.

"I will forget what has happened. I...I will forget all of you.

Let me get off at Moscow and I will say no more. Or if you like you can tie me up till you have made your escape."

His eyes rolled as he looked at each one of them in turn. He could tell that they were tempted to let him go. A few more minutes and they would have no recourse but to keep him on the train. "I promise."

His words, however, did not have too much sway except it pleased them all to hear him utter them. At last Petrov the secret policeman was showing signs of real fear. He looked down at the rushing ground just below the carriage and then further to the snow covered fields and barren woods. No sign of habitation for miles. Perhaps he might survive. He couldn't be too many miles from some human contact.

As if reading his thoughts, Irina suddenly pointed at him. "Take his coat off, and his jacket."

The student handed the policeman's heavy gun to Petrushka and quickly dragged the coat from Petrov, who allowed him to remove it without a struggle. "Now the jacket."

She jerked her own small gun at the already shivering figure of the secret policeman who, not daring to resist, undid it and handed it to the student.

"Outside with them."

The student then threw both the coat and the jacket through the doorway where they were caught by the wind of the passing train and spun away somewhere in the snow, to be found maybe later in the year by some local farmer or woodsman. He then took back the service revolver from Petrushka.

Petrov half glanced at the swirling clothing and could picture himself twisting and turning like a rag doll till he came to rest somewhere at the side of the track. His chances of survival had suddenly been considerably reduced. Even though spring was not far off, with temperatures below zero, he could not hope to remain alive for long. If later he were found it would still be too late. In any case who would be looking for him. He knew that in the final analysis he was expendable.

"It's still a better chance than you gave your victims,

Comrade Policeman, Irina said through tight lips turning blue with the cold. "Now it's your turn to follow your coat and jacket." She waved her small pistol at him but he just stood shivering in the open doorway.

"Shoot him and be done with it." The small, shabby man again expressed his impatience and anger. "Any chance is too much for the likes of him."

"Jump!" Irina ordered.

"Push him!" Olga screamed.

"Kick him out!" Natalia yelled.

"Shoot him," Petrushka urged again.

The student, who was behind Petrov, looked at Irina with doubt and uncertainty in his eyes. He didn't want to be the one.

She knew that and could understand his feelings. While the others were shouting their own encouragements to be heard above the roaring of the wind, Irina herself froze, not knowing what to do. But it was just for a moment and as she moved towards Petrov, a hand reached out from behind her, a hand holding a heavy service revolver. There was a jerk and a loud popping sound, dulled by the roaring wind.

Petrov convulsed into one monstrous spasm as the bullet smashed into his backbone. He tumbled from the carriage, bouncing down the slight slope, with blood spraying in tiny spots on the snow, till he came to rest out of sight among some tall reeds.

Irina and the student took a quick backward look but could see nothing. The grey mist of dawn had closed in behind them. The train sped onwards.

For a moment no one did anything till the cold, biting wind reminded them that the door of the carriage was still open. The student Mikhail and the small, shabby man Petrushka, struggled for a while against the wind until they had finally pulled the door closed with a heavy, almost comforting crunch. It was over and they all stood motionless and silent.

It was the conductress who made them suddenly aware of their precarious position as she came hustling back up the corridor.

"Is it finished now?" she asked in a nervous whisper.

Irina nodded. "It is finished, and you heard and saw nothing understand."

"I don't need reminding of that," the conductress snapped petulantly. "I had come to hate him as well, remember. My daughter is avenged at last."

Irina smiled wearily. "I was forgetting, comrade. I'm sorry."

"Now you must get back to your compartment. I have to wake these tourists, though with all this fuss I should be surprised if any of them are still asleep."

"No-one saw anything did they?" Natalia asked apprehensively.

The conductress shook her head. "No – I'm sure of it. I couldn't hear what was going on, so I'm certain they wouldn't. Besides, some of them were making their own noise. Kids, I hate them."

With that final comment she unlocked her own cabin and disappeared inside, no doubt to revive her nerves with a hearty swig of vodka.

The rest of the travellers made their way back to the compartment and to their original seats, where they were content to sit a while in silence.

Irina looked at her wristwatch. The time showed five forty-five. An hour or just a little more before they would be arriving in Leningrad Station, Moscow. Soon they would be seeing the first signs of habitation, the isolated wooden huts of local peasant farmers, or maybe something a little grander. Despite the frugality of their existence Irina had always envied them their isolation. Not like the big city flats, where everybody lived so close upon each other. She looked across at Petrushka and noted with alarm that he still had the policeman's pistol, which he had snatched from the hand of the student. "You should have got rid of it," she gasped.

Petrushka looked at the gun, heavy, black and silently menacing. He stroked the barrel in a kind of affection and then flicked open the bullet chamber and spun it noisily.

"If I had thrown it away at the same time as we threw away Comrade Petrov, there was always the possibility that it would be found, with one bullet fired. It is better that I keep it. If anyone is to be implicated, let it be me."

Irina could see the sense in what he said, "Very well. You are right I think. But if the occasion should arise when you might find yourself in trouble with the police again, I suggest that you make sure you dispose of that gun once and for all."

After that short exchange between Irina and the small, shabby man nothing was spoken for some time. The heavy atmosphere, which had pervaded the compartment for most of the journey, was lifted. In its place was nothing – just a silent emptiness. Outside, the dawn had turned into early morning and the vagueness of the landscape had now resolved itself into more definite images. The tall, straight pines stood out black and fearsome against the snow covered fields, while the birch dallied around the edges of the dark woods like a silver frill, somehow out of place in such an austere setting. When spring and summer overtook them then they would become entirely appropriate, with their soft green foliage mocking the grim straightness of their companions. That was for the future. Now it was very cold with snow still clinging to the ground and refusing to give way to the change of season. Further away, the early morning sunlight, now creeping over the horizon, sparkled on some distant ice-bound pool or lake, adding an extra brilliance to the growing day. Severe and daunting though this landscape may be, it was now less than fifty miles from Moscow.

If any of the travellers had taken the trouble to look out of the windows at the passing scene, they would have noticed a dwelling. It was a poor wooden offering as seen from the window of a moving train, yet it was sturdy and neat. It had survived the winter and emerged from the snows unscathed. The garden was substantial though not large, and it was neatly laid out. The snow had all but disappeared from this farmer's property, although the fields further away were still white. The house was old and belonged to a past age, with its fancy wooden gables and fairy-tale quaintness. It was a dull red in colour and when the winter was completely gone it would shine again, like its cousins in the Swiss Alps. To those in the passing carriages it was nothing special. It was just one of many such buildings that the traveller could expect to see when away from the big, grey cities of concrete and drabness. To the average Russian city dweller these kinds of places were merely remnants of a past decadence. Some were isolated, others in groups as now they began to flash past the windows in greater numbers.

None of this was of any particular significance to the travellers in that last compartment. Not even Olga was looking out of the window. She just sat staring in front of her, with her hands clasped in her lap-like a parody of some pagan idol. They were all lost in their own thoughts as they struggled to come to terms with the events of the past few hours.

Irina had slipped her own small gun into her shoulder bag. From the same bag she took a small pocket mirror and studied her face. The mark of Petrov's fist was beginning to turn into an ugly, blue-black bruise. Though she gingerly dabbed powder on her face it would still show. But it couldn't be helped. Casually and deliberately she then applied another layer of lipstick to restore her feminine looks. It was not possible that this woman could be in the same profession as the sinister Petrov, at least that was the image she intended to convey. When she had completed her restoration she leaned back against the padded seat and closed her eyes.

At the same time Petrushka, the small, shabby man next to Irina, was secreting the heavy black revolver, formerly owned by the policeman Petrov, somewhere on his person. Russian coats were so voluminous that there were always pockets, which did not present unsightly bulges. When he had done that he too leaned back against the padded seat and closed his eyes. He did not bother to check the cuts and bruises on his face, which had been sustained by his earlier encounters with the policeman Petrov. They were not important anyway. They hardly showed. Besides he needed a shave. It didn't look too bad on him. After all he didn't want to stand out as someone respectable or important. It was much too dangerous. It was safer to be as he was, so that he could pass unnoticed among the millions of others unwashed, unshaved and bruised. It would help him to survive and that's all that really mattered.

The young girl, Natalia, meantime had been re-wrapping her doll with the cracked face. It was important, for if she got on the train with a baby she should leave the train with one. Had it been a real child she could not have shown more care and tender motherly love for it. Gently she wrapped the coarse piece of blanket around it, ensuring at the same time that she disguised its doll-like shape and had built it up into a more acceptable contour. The grubby shawl added a final touch. Once more she sat back with her 'baby' clutched tight against her breast. She did not want to sleep yet. She did not feel tired. She just sat and stared and held onto her 'baby'.

The young student Mikhail sat doing nothing in particular. Now it was all over he seemed restless. He was still fully charged with nervous energy and the small compartment had all at once become too restricting. He found it difficult to sit still and just contemplate the future or relive the past, the recent past that is.

Olga, the square faced woman in the corner seat began to sift through her bag and arrange its contents in some sort of order. She had strangely lost all her former enthusiasm for looking out of the window. It was odd really for now there was something to look at. Occasionally she muttered something to herself but nobody took any notice. In fact nobody took any notice of anybody else. They might all have been strangers who had come together for the first time. They didn't even look at each other.

Meanwhile the train continued its journey with speed unabated. Outside in the corridor the conductress was patrolling to keep an eye on any of younger and more unruly of the tourists. Noises could be heard emanating from the region of the tourists' berths. Thumps and bangs denoted cases being manhandled and slid into the corridor in preparation. The five passengers in the last compartment had little of that sort of thing to worry about. Even the attractive Irina had managed to pack all she required into one small case. The others did not possess such a luxury. The student had had his rucksack; the other women were content with bags. The small, shabby man had nothing except that all embracing heavy coat of his. Soon they would all be arriving in Moscow together. The only passenger not to arrive was already many miles behind them, lying lifeless on the neglected edge of some farmer's field. He would not be discovered for some weeks and maybe not at all. That no longer concerned the group in that last compartment.

As the train drew ever nearer to its destination, their thoughts began to turn towards the future. In the event, those thoughts were interrupted as the conductress suddenly slid the door back and announced their expected arrival at Leningrad Station, Moscow in fifteen minutes.

Flying past the window was now a much different scene. Already they were in the outskirts of the great city of Moscow, ancient capital of Russia. Outside the carriage a confused tangle of buildings and structures were filling the view in an ever-changing pattern, as if the train itself were part of some gigantic kaleidoscope. Individual houses were fewer. Instead, great blocks of grey brick flats began to sprout up in place of the tall, dark pines. The sky was clear and the sun was bright. Vast stretches of the skyline were bathed in the early brightness and great new forests of grey, impersonal blocks had now supplanted the tall, graceful pines. It was with much difficulty that an individual dwelling could now be discerned. Whether they liked it or not, the average Muscovite had to make do with these tall, dull monuments to expediency and practicality. There may not have been the same beauty to behold in such a regulated forest of concrete, but by sheer profusion of numbers they compelled a sort of reverence. The reverence though should perhaps be reserved more for those who had the pure blind obstinacy to live in them. Somewhere in this jungle of concrete blocks all of the five passengers would find their own respective nests and would consider themselves lucky at that. If any of them aspired to a less Spartan domicile they kept it to themselves.

Sounds of laughter and shouts roused the five from their own individual reveries and instinctively they began to gather together their luggage. A few more minutes and they will have arrived in the heart of Moscow.

"We shall not meet again," said Irina, "and what has been accomplished by us is now buried in the past. I hope you all understand that. Keep out of the hands of the police. I cannot help you if for any reason you are picked up. Just wipe this episode from your minds."

She spoke mostly to Olga and the two young ones. She then turned to Petrushka.

"My only advice to you, Petrushka is to disappear. Never be found again. You cannot achieve more than you have already."

Petrushka nodded. He understood anonymity. He had lived under its cloak all his life.

There were no other parting words and Irina could tell that none were necessary. They all understood.

Somewhere up ahead, a sharp, nasal clarion from the engine signalled that they were approaching the station and the end of the journey. With coats buttoned up and hats firmly in place they eased their way into the corridor. For the last minute or two they stood uneasily, regarding this part as the most uncomfortable and longest of all the minutes spent on the night train.

Their presence was an occasion for the one or two tourists, also preparing for disembarkation, to give them curious stares. Though neither the native nor the tourist had spoken or fraternised in any way, they had nevertheless, had a common bond in that they had travelled together on the night train from Leningrad.

With a smooth, imperceptible slowing down the night train glided into the terminus of the Leningrad Station, and then to a halt. They had arrived in Moscow.

Chapter Fifteen
Leningrad Station - Moscow

The clock in the station showed a few minutes past seven in the morning. Below it, on a brand new modern gauge, the temperature in Moscow was revealed at zero degrees centigrade. The day was clear and the sky was blue. It was cold and fresh with all traces of dawn gloom dispelled in the ever-brightening sunshine.

The station itself is much the same as that at Leningrad but those who had occupied the last carriage would be aware that the canopy of glass and girder did not extend to the limit of the platform. There was also a greater sense of bustle and activity here in Moscow. But that could be because it was the beginning of a day and not the end of one. Trolleys with countless trailers were already charging down to the far reaches of the platform to gather the huge pile of suitcases and bags, which, within a few minutes of the train arriving, had been deposited by the excited tourists. In no time the cold air was punctuated by a host of foreign voices issuing orders, swapping jokes, complaining of the weather, asking directions and a hundred other sundry sounds that a group of tourists might make upon arrival at a new place on their itinerary. If talk and chatter were the prerequisites for the tourists then a railway station was the ideal place to conduct such banter. Later they would be subdued to reverential whispers as they visited the spectacular delights that lay in store. For now, their chatter added to the growing noise and tumult of a great station and helped to create an air of excitement and anticipation.

The five Russian travellers from the last compartment of the last carriage were first off the train, as soon as the conductress opened the door. As they left they nodded to her but exchanged no words. That is the way she wanted it. She was glad they were gone, for until they had left she knew that the business was not really complete. The five travellers did not talk to each other nor did they give any sign of parting. They mingled in the growing crowd as they proceeded up the platform towards the head of the train and the exit of the station.

Olga, the square faced woman, with the square shaped body, trundled swiftly through the thickening crowd with the skill of one well used to the ways of a city. She spent little effort on being good mannered. She heaved and shoved when she thought it was necessary, which was often. As she hurried towards the exit she had only one thought on her mind and that was to get away as quickly as possible. The train was a minute or so late she judged but she knew that the person waiting to meet her outside would wait. In those final, feverish steps her mind transported itself back to the beginning of the journey and she could not help grinning to herself.

'I'm glad that's over. I thought that journey would never end. Anyway he deserved what he got for humiliating me like that. I would have done away with him myself. I wasn't afraid of him. How I hated him for showing me up. Those policemen are all the same. I'll bet that blonde is the same at heart. Only pretended to be on my side because it suited her. They're not very clever, these policemen after all. He thought he knew everything. He knew nothing about anybody. I enjoyed the way we fooled him with those roubles and other things. It was good to see the look on his face. Ha! I must get out of here quickly. If I don't hurry I will miss my contact. There are so many people. Anyway I shan't see that lot again that's for certain. And next time I go on that train it will be in the daytime. Why are there so many people here at this time of the day? Must hurry. Serves him right. I wonder when he'll be found - if he ever is found. Still, there's nothing to connect me with it. I made sure of that. Policemen are so stupid, all of them. That one didn't even bother to search me. He should have done. He would have found the real money. My money. Served him right. Huh. If he'd laid a hand on that he would have found himself dealing with a different sort of person. I wouldn't have let him get that far. He would have found out what it was like to get into a real fight. They're mine. I worked for them. Why shouldn't I do what I like with my own money? What business is it of his whether I sell them or not? I know a few people. Only take me a year I reckon before I've got a nice tidy sum. I hope that lad's here. The quicker I can get started the quicker I can make my pile. I deserve it. I've had to go without long enough because of that stupid husband of mine. I wonder what he's doing these days. In gaol I shouldn't wonder. Now there's a character for that policeman. I'd like to see how they'd get on together. Yes, that should be something. But all that's in the past. Money - when I get enough I'll get out of here. Go to the Black Sea. Go somewhere. I wonder if I could get out of Russia. They say that money can buy anything. Well if that's the case I'm going to make plenty. Policemen! Ha! Fools! They know nothing about the likes of me.'

Olga, with head and shoulders hunched, trundled like a small tank through the swirling crowds towards the exit. Her square, stocky frame crashed unceremoniously into any group of tourists who were unfortunate enough to be in her way. She reckoned that they had no right to be there flaunting their expensive, flashy western clothes and luggage. Wait till she had money. Just wait. These were the sentiments, which she muttered to herself over and over, her jaw set grimly towards the future. The past was forgotten as soon as she emerged from the Leningrad Station and scuttled into the streets of Moscow, where she became indistinguishable from the countless, drab, uninspiring figures, which hurried in quiet fervour about their various enterprises. A Russian city was no place for an idler, unless a tourist of course.

Somewhere else among the bustling crowds, Mikhail the student was also making his way along the endless platform. The five erstwhile travellers had the furthest to go having been in the last carriage of the train. It seemed an age before he could reach an exit. There was too much time in which to reflect on the events of the night. He still found it difficult to grasp what had happened and as he walked as rapidly as the crowds would allow, he thought that his legs might give way. They felt so weak. On the whole he reckoned that it had all gone well.

'I can't believe it. I just can't believe it. Still, I don't want to go through all that again. I'm glad that scruffy little man killed him. I wanted to. I've never been so certain about anything in my life but I didn't fancy being the executioner. Then I would have been the one with most to lose. I don't suppose he will be found for months yet, if he is found at all. No one will be able to connect any of us with his death. Huh! What a fool that policeman was. Big and ugly, and devious, but he was still a fool. I can't imagine why he didn't search my luggage or me. Fancy relying on those packets I gave him. It was all too easy. He swallowed our stories without any real evidence to back them. If that's the quality of the secret police, guarding the nation's secrets, then he is better out of the way. I wonder why that woman didn't shoot him. I thought that was the plan. Still it all worked out for the best. I shall be glad to get out of this station. Why are the crowds so dense today and why are there so many tourists? I shouldn't complain. I need the tourists. They're the ones with the American dollars and German marks. Moscow is just the place. I'll be glad to get into the city and away from the station. That's one thing for certain. I shan't be travelling to Leningrad again, not by the overnight train anyway. Why did he say those things to me I wonder, about my friends - girl friends and not boy friends. How did he know? How could he have been so sure? I don't like him – didn't like him. I don't want to think about him. I just want to get on with my life and forget all about that business. Grandfather Alex has been avenged and that's all that matters. I'm glad. That policeman was such a fool though. I can't help smiling just to think of him believing that I would hand over real drugs, just like that. A good job he didn't search though. For a while I was worried. If he had just looked into my rucksack, like he did that woman's bag, I would have been in a spot. Nicolai would not have been pleased with me, nor could I have made any money. That policewoman would have taken them I bet. A woman is always harder than a man. I wonder why she didn't shoot him. Odd that. Still it's all over now. I've still got my stuff. That's worth a few uncomfortable hours. What a fool!'

So Mikhail, the one time radical student, alternately consoled and congratulated himself on his cleverness and good fortune as he rapidly made his way through the crowds. He paused as he drew near to any group of tourists and slowly sauntered past them, trying to pick out likely customers. He hesitated as he wondered whether now was the right time to make his approaches. Most of the western tourists were about his age, and he already knew from his experience and dealings in Leningrad that there were always one or two in any group who might be prepared to buy or sell something. If it wasn't drugs it could easily be clothes or jewellery, Mikhail didn't mind what it was. He could always trade anything for the real stuff of life. On the platform, however, nobody seemed too interested in a loitering Russian youth. They were all much too busy and anxious to be moving off the platform and out of the station. For the tourists the great excitement at the moment was to explore the city of Moscow. Mikhail could wait. The streets of this city were paved with unsuspecting tourists these days and it wouldn't take him too long to run into them. As he had already discovered in Leningrad, some of them were only too willing to do business, any sort of business. He often used to think that was the only reason they came to Russia. It was his ambition to see that they went home satisfied while he remained that much richer. Quickly he made for the exit and soon he was lost among the throng.

The young girl Natalia had played the part of the young mother well but it was now becoming irksome. She allowed a porter to help her with her bag till she had found a seat further along the platform. There she sat, claiming that she expected someone to meet her. She needed to rest and gather her wits before resuming her life. Though everything had gone according to plan, she still felt very shaky and rather tired. She had been a long time without sleep. Even so she would be glad to be off this platform and out of the station. She must also get rid of the 'child' in her arms. It had served its purpose but now it was an embarrassment and a nuisance. She needed to drop it somewhere. She looked around at the milling crowds and tried to think of a likely place. She could not afford to undo the charade in public. It would have to be somewhere secluded - the ladies' toilet was a likely place. Still playing the part of the mother she began to make her way towards the main building of the station, all the time thinking that she would be heartily pleased when she was out of here.

'I must find somewhere to dump this wretched doll. Too many people are looking at me. They make me nervous. People always make me nervous, and I don't want to go through all that again. I don't think I could. It's a good job that the others didn't realise how ill I really was. I should have been resting after that operation. Still it all worked out well enough. How I hated that policeman. I can't honestly say that I'm sorry for what has happened. He had only himself to blame. If only he hadn't picked on us he might still be alive. It's too late now. I'm glad he's dead. He deserved it. He was too clever. He knew too much about the inside of a person. I don't like those kinds of people. Always looking at you and trying to work out what is wrong with you and what you like or don't like; all about your private life, thoughts and feelings. How would he know anyway? He's not a woman. He doesn't know what it's like to be a mother. Well I do, at least I would have done, if I'd decided to go through with it. I did it for Boris. He gave me the money so I suppose he's got a right to decide whether he wanted the baby or not. How I hated that policeman! Why couldn't he have left us alone? Now it's all over, and I'm not going to weep any tears for him. I hope they never find him. I must get rid of this thing in my arms. It's strange, but at times I thought that I had a real baby. I wonder what it would have been like to have had a real baby with me on the journey. One thing's certain - I wouldn't have let that policeman come near it. Yes - I wonder what a real live baby would have been like. I shan't know now. Boris will be pleased. I hope he will meet me outside. He'd better. I've gone through a lot of trouble for him but I shall only tell him about the operation. Funny to see the look on his face when I told him I was pregnant. Frightened him to death. Good job my parents don't know. It's best that way. Ah! Here's a place.'

Natalia had reached a sort of sanctuary, a dull, grey building and quickly disappeared inside. She emerged a little while later quite a different woman. Gone was the white bundle, which she had held so suffocatingly close to her for the last ten hours. No longer was she the wide-eyed, nervous young girl. Some sparse but judicial make-up had enlivened her features and without the bundle there was now more elegance and assurance in her step. She did not linger but made straight for the exit, where she spotted the young man she had hoped would be meeting her. Her steps quickened and soon she was clutching his arm and dragging him away. Then in no time they had disappeared amongst the crowd.

The small, shabby man, the one called Petrushka, took his time about leaving. He wanted to see that the others got well away. It was not their welfare he was concerned with but his own. He wanted to be sure that no one who knew him would see him blend into the background of the city. There wasn't anybody to meet him, of that he was certain. He too was glad the experiences of the night were over. He had had other more frightening experiences but none quite so strange as this one. As he slipped from the train he glanced at the conductress. She looked straight past him as though he hadn't been there. That was good, he thought. He wanted to be forgotten as soon as possible. He needed to go carefully, especially with the policeman's gun in his pocket. He knew that he was a wanted man and could easily be picked up anytime. That was for the future, not yet. Slowly he ambled along the platform. This was the worst part for him because he stood out amongst the brightly smart tourists who were banded together around great mountains of luggage, which even now was being crammed onto long series of trolleys to be conveyed to waiting coaches. He wished he could hide himself among these tourists for an hour or so. It least it would get him out of the station. As he tried to walk casually towards the exit, where the crowds were thickest, he reflected on the changing features of the past twenty-four hours. He had to admit to himself it was all a very chancy business.

'I don't think I want to go through that lot again. Getting caught was bad enough, and that was no easy matter. I must have stalked that Petrov for days before I could arrange my capture. He is such a dolt. Though maybe I'm being too critical. After all I only get caught if it suits my purpose. I can't say that I'll lose any sleep over his loss. Good riddance! He deserved to die if anyone did. He nearly got away from us too. If I hadn't snatched the gun and pulled the trigger we could never have been certain. I like to be certain. Females are all very well but you can't rely on them for a job like that, even if she is in the service. She would have let him go. And the others - huh. They hadn't a clue. He'll rot there I reckon. It will be pure luck if he is found soon. If he is found the authorities will have no idea which train he came from. Not that they will bother too much with him, I'm sure of that. They all took such a time and they never did really break him. I don't think he believed, not until he saw his coat flying out there in the wind. The look on his face then was worth something. I could have laughed out loud. I'm glad the bastard's dead. Funny though that he should have thought I was this Petrushka. Got the name wrong I suppose. Russians are like that. All sound the same to some people, especially to idiots like that Petrov. Well that's over and done with, now let's get out of this station before some other idiot policeman gets ambitious. I must get a shave and smarten up a bit. Would attract less attention I suppose. Get some new clothes now I've got a bit of money. I wonder if I'll get another job like that one? I don't mind a few knocks if the pay is right. I wonder who that Petrushka is though - seemed important to the policeman. I should like to meet him sometime.'

The small, shabby man had ambled and shuffled his way to the main building without being accosted by anyone, but then he was not likely to know that instructions had already been given that he was not to be molested in anyway by the authorities. He was to be allowed to make his way into the streams of people pouring out of Leningrad Station, where his shabbiness was not so obvious. He blended in perfectly with the crowd like a shuffling chameleon.

Irina had watched her executioner all the way from the train. She wanted to be sure that he had no trouble in getting into the city streets. Despite the small man's misgivings, she had been aware from the beginning that it would be he who was likely to squeeze the trigger and not her. She was secretly glad of that fact for she would rather have not had to be the one to do it. At last it was all over and the little man having played his part was now vanishing into obscurity. Irina knew that there would be a car waiting for her somewhere. The job had been a complete success although it seemed at times that Petrov might have got away. There was never any chance of that. She would quite happily have killed him without the pantomime. But it was necessary she supposed.

Slowly she walked the length of the platform, pausing to allow several groups of tourists to push excitedly past her. She had held back till the last, pretending to get off then slipping into another compartment. She had wanted to speak to the conductress as well as to make sure that they all got out of the station without any incident. Once on the streets of Moscow it was up to themselves. She was not answerable for them in the city. The early morning coldness made her face tingle and she was conscious of the soreness caused by that blow. She had known worse but it was just one more thing to add to the list of Petrov's crimes against people. He just had to go. Even her bosses had recognised that fact. He was out of date as was the rest of his kind. It was over and she was glad of it. She wanted no more assignments like that. It was all much too theatrical and much too risky. She smiled a wry smile as she approached the station buildings and could glimpse the large black limousine waiting just outside the gates. It was hers. She knew that. No one else had arrived on the night train that would warrant or command such treatment. The secret police were very powerful and sometimes made no secret of what that power can mean. She thought the whole episode rather ironical and perhaps a little sad. There was no doubt that Petrov got what he deserved but she wasn't so sure about the others. They all seemed to be too simple, too straightforward. Was Petrov right about them she wondered? And she began to wonder about other things.

'I wonder of he is still waiting for me. I can't tell him about myself. Worse, I suppose, was that I used him, but he doesn't really know that. In fact he doesn't really know anything. I can see him now, pacing about the flat, looking for a note. I wished I had left one for him, something, some message. I wished I could - No. That would be too silly and too dangerous. Maybe I could get back and see him before he leaves. Maybe he will come to Moscow. He will have to leave the flat soon anyway. It is only rented for the month. Such a strange business it all is. It is no good worrying or supposing or wishing. It can never be. I must be content with memories. Ah! I see my driver approaching. I bet he's surprised to see me dressed like this. Davidaniya Englishman - we may meet again. Who knows.'

For a brief second or two Irina looked along the length of the platform she had just walked; at the train and the track, which carried all the way back to Leningrad. For now she wanted to forget that journey but someday she might remember. All she wanted to remember was Leningrad, where she had met the Englishman. She smiled and fingered her wristwatch as she remembered for the last time the man who had given it to her. 'For services rendered' she would put in her report.

Her driver saluted and opened the door of the sleek, black limousine. Soon the attractive Irina was swallowed up like the others in the bustle of the great city of Moscow.

At the same time the sundry groups of tourists were boarding their coaches to be whisked away to some lavish hotel in a distant part of the city. Later, much later, they too would remember with a different kind of nostalgia, their own journey on the night train from Leningrad.